Carol Marinelli recently filled in a form asking for her job title. Thrilled to be able to put down her answer, she put 'writer'. Then it asked what Carol did for relaxation, and she put down the truth—'writing'. The third question asked for her hobbies. Well, not wanting to look obsessed, she crossed her fingers and answered 'swimming'—but, given that the chlorine in the pool does terrible things to her highlights, I'm sure you can guess the real answer!

FORBIDDEN TO THE POWERFUL GREEK

CAROL MARINELLI

MILLS & BOON

First published in Great Britain 2022
by Mills & Boon, an imprint of HarperCollins*Publishers* Ltd,
1 London Bridge Street, London, SE1 9GF

www.harpercollins.co.uk

HarperCollins*Publishers*
1st Floor, Watermarque Building,
Ringsend Road, Dublin 4, Ireland

Large Print edition 2022

ISBN: 978-0-263-29528-3

06/22

MIX
Paper from
responsible sources
FSC
www.fsc.org **FSC® C007454**

This book is produced from independently certified FSC™ paper to ensure responsible forest management. For more information visit www.harpercollins.co.uk/green.

Printed and Bound in the UK using 100% Renewable Electricity at CPI Group (UK) Ltd, Croydon, CR0 4YY

PROLOGUE

'WHAT HAVE THEY done to you now?'

Almost thirty years ago, six-year-old Galen Pallas had heard the weariness in his *yaya*'s tone as he'd stepped in their home high on the hilly Greek island of Anapliró.

Galen's shorn black hair had been full of mud, his clothes torn and his face bruised, so there had been no denying that there had once again been trouble...

And, again, it had seemed it was all his faut.

'Galen!' Yaya had been cross when she'd found out the reason the boys had again ganged up on him—and she'd blamed Galen. 'You don't tell your teacher that she's got bigger after the summer.'

'She said it to me, though...' Galen had frowned. It was the first thing everyone said when they saw him!

Yaya had turned from the stove and held her hands apart. 'I meant you don't comment on someone's size...' Yaya had looked skywards for guidance and muttered some prayers. 'I am too old for this...'

'I didn't say it to them, though,' he'd pointed out, 'just the teacher.'

'They are boys being boys and you provoke

them. Trust me on this,' Yaya had insisted. 'Sometimes it is better to say nothing, or even to lie. Your first thought, your first response, is not always the appropriate one. Galen, you offend people...'

With the table laid Yaya had brought over dinner, and though Galen had closed his eyes as they'd said prayers, his mind had been somewhere else, and as she'd started to serve he'd told Yaya the truth. 'I would never kick someone, or spit on them, or call them names, no matter how much they offended me.'

And they offended him daily! Calling him a *rompot*, or robot, for his undemonstrative ways. Laughing because he lived in the hills with his *trelós yaya* as they all called her. Yes, she was eccentric, and she wept in church, and at times openly on the street. Galen knew she was almost demented with grief at the loss of her family. His *papu* had died before Galen had been born, and when he had been two Galen had been in an accident that had claimed his parents.

Yaya had been left to raise him and, as he was frequently told, it was not an easy task.

'Galen, you are different...'

He watched how Yaya's glass of water trembled as she brought it to her mouth, and he hated the trouble he caused her. 'You need to think before you speak *every* time. You want to fit in, don't you?'

As a child, and later as a teenager, Galen simply hadn't.

Oh, but as a man…

His brilliant brain had soon been so in demand that the world had rather quickly decided it might be wiser, as well as extremely profitable, if it chose to fit in with him.

CHAPTER ONE

'GALEN.' HIS PA placed a large take-out coffee on his desk, though it went unacknowledged for he was deep in his work. 'Sorry to interrupt, but Costa keeps calling—says you were supposed to be meeting him and Leo for dinner at V's?'

The restaurant was opposite Galen's head office in Kolonaki Square, a very upmarket neighbourhood in Athens. Both he and Costa had bought, and now worked from, the once dilapidated building. Their businesses were separate entities, though—Costa was into property, and Galen's passion was technology. And right now, he was exceptionally busy.

'No,' Galen said. 'I've told him I can't make it.'

'Sure.'

'Kristina!' Galen called her back. 'The care home called this morning with the treatment regime?'

'Yes,' she nodded. 'It's on the report.'

'I just saw.' Galen took a breath. Had she told him about Yaya he would have gone over today. Then again, he had insisted on not being disturbed and the care home did call a *lot*. 'Let me know if it's regarding treatment.'

'Noted.'

He heard the slightly tired edge to her tone, reminding him that she was heavily pregnant. 'Go home?' he suggested.

'I don't need favours.'

'It's not a favour. We've got a busy weekend coming up and I want you fully on board.'

Galen was by most accounts brilliant…mathematically, technically, fiscally… As for his looks…he was way more than the requisite tall dark and handsome, with intense hazel eyes and an incredible body. His thick black hair, when he had time, was superbly cut. Even by Athens' high standards, he dressed impeccably.

Not that he cared for fashion. His mind was filled with more important things.

Numbers. Food. Sex. Or numbers. Sex. Food.

Most of the time it was just numbers.

Charts.

Code.

Programming…

Galen didn't notice the lights going off outside his glass office—he had blacked out the glass. Nor them coming back on as the cleaning team arrived—they knew not to come into his office when he was deep in work.

There were many satellites that orbited Galen's world—legal, admin, social media, maintenance… The list went on, but Galen loathed all the distractions they created so, in as far as it was possible, they orbited his world offsite.

Onsite, though, aside from the developers, quants, programmers and such, was a small vital army who, apart from one very lazy exception, worked away all the days and nights so that Galen and the team could immerse themselves in tech.

And, yes, while Galen's brilliance might pay an awful lot of wages, at the core they were a very loyal and exceptionally devoted team to their aloof, at times arrogant and rather remote boss.

A short rap on his door had him frowning, but he remained immersed in work until he heard his name. 'Galen.'

'What?' Galen sighed when he saw that it was Costa. 'I already said I can't get there…' Though come to think of it he was a little hungry. 'Maybe a quick dinner.'

'Galen, it's almost midnight.'

'Oh!' He had long since lost track of time.

V's generally did not do take-out, but there were always exceptions, and Costa handed over a container. 'Here.'

'Thanks.'

The chef would probably weep as his carefully prepared lamb tenderloins drizzled in his signature sauce, with delectable baby potatoes and a delicate side salad, were all scooped onto a piece of pitta and rolled up as Costa asked, 'How's it all going?'

'Do you want the long or the short answer?'

Galen asked, because he was more than aware now of how people's eyes tended to glaze over when he spoke of his work.

'I won't understand either of them,' Costa admitted. 'The drift...'

'Well, the first of the ICOs went well.'

'You've already lost me.' Costa grinned.

'Initial coin offerings. Although there is still...'

Galen saw that Costa had tuned out, so he took a large bite of his wrap, but then frowned as Costa produced from a bag a bottle of champagne and two glasses.

'What's this?' Galen checked, hastily swallowing as Costa popped the cork. 'Are you going to tell me you love me, Costa?' he joked. 'Because if you are, then it really has to wait. I need a clear head to work...'

'Galen, I've got news,' Costa said, handing him a glass and then sitting down.

'Okay...'

'*Good* news,' Costa said—and, yes, he was telling him how to react, Galen realised. 'Mary and I are getting married.'

'Mary?' Galen frowned. Frankly, he couldn't quite keep up with Costa's love life, but Mary was the most recent one. 'You're serious?' Galen checked. 'But you only recently met...'

He was more than a touch bemused. It had nothing to do with his own views on relationships and marriage, more that Costa really wasn't the settling down type. Still, even though Galen was actually itching to get back to work, it was indeed good news and so, remembering his manners, he halted his own impatience and raised his glass. *'Yamas...'*

'Yamas.' Costa shared in the toast and then put down his glass. 'Galen,' Costa said. 'I'd like you to be my *koumbaros.'*

'Me?' Costa was asking him to be his best man. 'Doesn't that involve speeches and…?'

'Yes.' Costa nodded. 'Speeches and dancing and being Mr Sociable and everything you hate…' Costa smiled. 'Look, we go back for ever. Long before…' He gestured to the *very* sumptuous surroundings. 'Of course it has to be you.'

'Well…' Galen blinked. 'Thank you.' He was both stunned and flattered, yet a little uncertain as to whether this was…well… A set-up. This was Costa after all! 'So…' Galen checked the little he knew about the sudden bride-to-be. 'Mary's English?'

'Yes.'

'Will you get married there?'

'It's still a bit up in the air…' Costa was toying with the champagne cork. 'I'm hoping the service will take place at my hotel in London.' Costa was very guarded to most, yet now he shared a confidence with Galen. 'Mary's father is in prison there; I'm trying to get his leave approved and surprise her.'

'I do have a good lawyer in the UK...' Galen offered.

'I've already pinched him,' Costa freely admitted. 'Anyway, the plan is to marry there, spend whatever time we can with her father, then fly back to Anapliró for a church blessing and reception.'

Galen felt his guts tighten a touch even at the mention of the island. He had left as a teenager and had, of course, gone back to visit Yaya. But she was now in a nursing home here, close by, and had been for years.

Galen felt neither the need nor the desire to return to Anapliró.

In fact, he hated the place.

Still—his analytical mind ticked over—he had to deal with the family home there, which was no doubt going to ruin. It was one of those jobs he'd been putting off, but this wedding might be a good time to put things in motion.

'A big Anapliró celebration, then.' Galen commented, trying to keep his mind on the conversation and wedding plans and all the things that just did not interest him. But when it came to friends, he had trained himself to listen.

'No,' Costa corrected. 'Without Mary's father that's not fair, so I'm keeping the reception to twelve and that includes us...' He gestured to Galen.

'And the bride,' Galen added.

'Indeed, and then there's Leo and Deacon, Yolanda of course...' She was Costa's mother. 'Your plus one.'

'I shan't be bringing anyone,' Galen said—not that Costa was listening.

He could not believe he was sitting here discussing Costa's wedding. The two men were both seriously single. Well, in different ways. Costa dated and borrowed Galen's PA to make bookings and to send flowers when it all invariably went wrong. As for Galen... Well, suffice it to say there were no flowers required when it was simply sex. And while that might appear cold, both Galen and his partners would contest that assumption—not that they cared what others thought.

In fact, his phone was buzzing now.

'I thought your calls were being diverted to Kristina.' Costa frowned. 'I've been trying to get you all night...'

Galen offered no explanation as he read the message and saw that it was one of his partners.

Catch up?

Galen fired a rapid response.

Can't now.

He added a sad face to his message.

And received a sad face in response.

His sex life really was as delightfully uncomplicated as that.

Right now, though, he dragged his focus onto Costa, who seemed to have everything planned.

'I'm going to offend a lot of people by keeping the reception small,' Costa admitted. 'But there will be a big party on the beach afterwards for everyone on the island—'

'Pias to avgo kai kourefto.' Galen shrugged. It literally meant grab an egg and shave it, but it referred more to the *Catch-22* situation Costa was in. 'It's not your job to please everyone. And anyway, that's an impossible ask on Anapliró.'

'Yes, well, I need to keep the locals happy, given that I didn't sever all ties like you.' Indeed, Costa had both masterminded and financed the development of a lavish retreat there. Once the impoverished poor relation of the islands, Anapliró was now an exclusive destination for the extremely well heeled. 'You still haven't seen the retreat.'

'I know,' Galen said. Costa had long since been pushing for him to fly over, yet Galen, thankfully, had always managed to be too busy. Yes, a trip to Anapliró was long overdue, and of course he would not miss Costa's wedding just because he loathed the place. 'When are you looking at?' Galen asked. 'I will ensure everything is cleared in my schedule…'

'Galen,' Costa said, and he tapped the champagne cork on the desk a few times, 'the wedding is on Saturday.'

'Excuse me?' Galen had long ago been taught not to not say the first thing that came to mind and rapidly deployed his filter rather than shaking his head and stating the truth—*that's impossible!*

'Yes.' Costa nodded. 'We fly to London tomorrow, the wedding is the following morning, and we go back to Anapliró that afternoon.' Costa took a breath. 'I know it's short notice…'

Short notice?

There was absolutely no way Galen could be there. He had to make a major announcement regarding a partnership on Saturday. And there were vital system updates to be checked and run. Every hour between now and then was accounted for.

Even sex was being forfeited!

While Galen didn't expect Costa's nuptials to be arranged around his schedule, in the same vein Costa was more than aware of the importance of the coming days for him.

'Galen,' Costa said into the ensuing silence, 'as God-awful as the timing is for you, believe me when I say there is a reason the wedding is

so soon and it's *not* the one you are thinking—
Mary isn't pregnant.'

'Why would I be thinking that?'

Costa laughed, but then he took a drink. Putting down the glass, he let out a sigh. 'There's
stuff going on...'

Hearing the sudden gravity in Costa's voice,
Galen frowned.

'Heavy stuff. But I honestly can't discuss it...'

'That's fine.' Galen was the least nosey person.
Drama and gossip irritated him, and certainly he
would never delve.

'I'm really asking you to be there.'

For many reasons Galen couldn't be, and yet...

Galen and Costa went way back.

Leo Arati too.

While they might all be successful now, in their
own rights, it hadn't always been so. They shared
a past only those who came from Anapliró could
understand.

Conform or suffer—that had been the unvoiced
motto of Anapliró.

All three, in their various ways, had refused
the former and endured the latter. If you weren't
one of the bullies or one of the popular crowd...
if you were in any way different...then your life
was made hell.

Costa's father had left when Yolanda had fallen

ill, and his parents' had been the island's first divorce.

Leo had suffered dreadfully—ostensibly for being tiny, but really for his effeminate ways.

And Galen, well…

They were unlikely friends, perhaps, but friends all the same, and that mattered.

'You know I'll be there…' Galen said, and there was another clink of glasses—and a smile—as his brain asked, *What the hell?* 'I'll message Kristina now…sort out…' He halted. Usually he would fire his PA messages at all hours, and yet, despite appearances, he *was* mindful that her due date was nearing.

'It's all done.' Costa waved him away. 'Flights and everything. London's booked and you've got the Temple Suite on Anapliró—it's amazing… the best on the retreat.'

'Shouldn't that go to the bride and groom?' Galen frowned.

'My villa's actually better.' He grinned and topped up Galen's glass.

'Of course it is.'

'I've put Leo and Deacon down for the bridal suite.'

'I'm sure that will be appreciated.'

'Hey, why not stay on for a few days…?'

'I shan't be joining you on your honeymoon, Costa.'

'I wasn't inviting you to, but it's been years since you've been back and—'

'There's nothing there for me now, and no reason to return,' Galen abruptly cut in. 'Your wedding is the exception.'

A very inconvenient exception at that!

The moment Costa left Galen began firing urgent messages to Joe and his development team, telling them to get here *now*. And, despite the late hour, he sent a quick one to Kristina, asking her to pack, and also to send his usual brief to both the London hotel and the retreat, so they were prepared to his specifications.

And also, in regard to Anapliró...

Ensure a good Internet connection!

Costa had said the retreat was amazing and that it had every luxury, but Galen had grown up there after all. It had been beyond poor then.

Merda! His announcement on Saturday wasn't just big—it had been timed for maximum impact.

Everything had been factored in...

Except for a damned wedding!

CHAPTER TWO

ROULA DRAKOS WAS rather certain she had the best office in the world.

Well, not her *actual* office. But often in her working day she paused to admire the endless theatre of the sky merging into the Aegean Sea. In the five years she had worked there the beauty and grandeur of the retreat still held her enthralled…

Still, there was no time to pause today.

She clipped at pace towards Reception and breezed into her *actual* office. Sitting down at her desk for the first time since she had arrived at work, Roula Drakos, Guest Services Manager, retrieved her to-do list from her rather untidy desk. She pushed a stray red curl out of her eyes and, snapping off a piece of her favourite dark chocolate, scrolled through the guest requests to ensure all had been met and found she was smiling at the sight of an old friend's name.

Galen Pallas plus one

Familiar faces were not particularly frequent amongst the guests here as Anapliró had once been very poor. Though locals often returned to the island, very few could afford to stay at the retreat.

Leo Arati was a renowned fashion designer, and he was here regularly, but Galen...

No.

She knew that he was friends with the owner, Costa, but Roula hadn't seen her old friend for... she thought back...nineteen years.

Well, they hadn't been friends, exactly. Galen had been several years older. But he had always been so kind to her.

She'd been Roula Kyrios then.

It really had been a lifetime ago.

'Roula.' The receptionist's rather loud rap on her door had her looking up. 'They're just leaving Thira.'

'Thanks.' Roula nodded. 'Is everything okay out there?'

'Mia's getting a little...' Stephanie made a wavering gesture with her hand that indicated the retreat's head chef was having her customary pre-function meltdown.

'So what's new?' Roula gave a nonchalant shrug and as always appeared unfazed. For the past thirty-six hours—since the news as to the identity of the bride and more pertinently the groom had been revealed—Roula had being doing her best to calm the staff, reminding them that although the groom was their boss, ultimately it was just another high-end wedding. Anapliró was now a very coveted destination and the retreat had seen many weddings, from royalty, to billionaire tycoons, to seriously wealthy celebrities.

'Let me finish this update and then I'll come by the kitchen.'

'Thanks.'

Roula wouldn't usually be flying quite so solo today. However, Yolanda, the retreat's manager, was also the groom's mother, and Beatrice, the wedding co-ordinator, was overseeing the London event.

Roula wore many hats.

Professional Roula was unflappable, breezy and efficient, and her focus was always on the guests. That was why in the five years since her husband's death she had moved through the ranks and was now Guest Services Manager.

She was gunning for Head of Guest Services—a role that Yolanda had pointed out did not exist.

Yet!

Her professional persona was by far the most comfortable fit—here she was completely in control. Her thick curly red hair was clipped back, and she wore subtle make-up and a neutral shade on her nails as was the policy. Her uniform consisted of a stone-coloured linen suit and a pale top, which she wore with heels or ballet pumps as required. She was poised and groomed right down to the requisite pearls in her ears and she wore her name badge with pride.

Her legs were toned and smooth, her figure for the most part trim, and yet beneath the coiffed appearance she was somewhat neglected. Roula could barely stand to be naked and always showered hurriedly, quickly taking care of the essentials. Even alone in the bathroom she put her underwear on beneath a towel, pulling on vast knickers and ensuring her large breasts were flattened by two sports bras before she emerged.

Nobody really knew Roula...

Updating the data to reflect that all suites were up to standard, she caught sight of her wedding ring—of course it was not a requirement of the retreat that she wore it...more a silent policy here on Anapliró. There was no question that she remove it. Eyebrows had already been raised when, a year after Dimitrios's death, Roula had stopped wearing black.

Seeing that the plaster on her thumb was fraying, she took a fresh one from the drawer to replace it. Roula had thought she'd kicked her nail-biting habit, but since her twenty-ninth birthday celebration it had resurfaced—though at least it was confined to one thumb nowadays.

'Roula!'

She looked up at the anxious calling of her name as Mia flew through the door.

'It's a disaster.'

'Mia.' They had been best friends growing

up—although, to Mia's chagrin, they weren't as close now. Still, with her professional hat on, Roula poured Mia a glass of water then waved her to a seat. 'Sit down.'

'I haven't got time to sit down.'

'I'm sure your staff have it all under control…'

'How can a wedding with less than thirty-six hours' notice ever be under control?'

'Believe me…' Roula rolled her eyes. 'I get it. Come on, you can take two minutes.'

'This is our *boss*. It's the most important meal of my career…'

Roula halted her. 'It's Costa. We were at school with him. He likes burgers…' Roula reminded her. 'He orders souvlaki at midnight—not from your kitchen, but from the stalls down at the tourist beach.'

'Yes…' Mia had finally sat down and was taking deeper breaths now. 'But his guests are all high-end and…'

'Leo?' Roula rolled her eyes. 'Come, now. Yes, he's famous now, but we have lunch with him on Santorini and the two of you go clubbing. He's a friend, and anyway I've made sure he has his favourite tipple. Who else are you worried about?'

'Galen Pallas and his guest.' Mia gulped.

'You honestly think that Galen is going to cause problems?'

'He's mega important now!'

'Please…' Roula shrugged. 'Galen invented that digital game my nieces play on.'

'He does way more than that…he's some tech guru…' Mia's gestured helplessly. 'He's seriously powerful and…'

'Come off it,' Roula dismissed. 'I remember Galen when he thought jam was a treat. He's the least of your worries. Mia, you have cooked for royalty, you have cooked for celebrities, you have more awards and stars than the website can keep up with and you can *absolutely* do a perfect wedding lunch for twelve.'

Mia finally took a deep breath.

'Twelve,' Roula reiterated.

'So, why didn't Costa want me to cater for the beach party?' the easily offended Mia asked. 'Does he not think I'm up to it?'

'It's a barbecue on the beach. The whole island is invited and they want you there for the party as a guest,' Roula said. 'You just have to hand over your kitchen to the Santorini chefs and have some fun. Just focus on the lunch, and some meze for the private guests after the beach party…'

'Yes.' Mia was breathing again. 'God, how do you hold it together, Roula? You're always so in control.'

'It's my job to be,' Roula said, and she had found out she was very good at it. 'You've got this.'

'I do.' Mia nodded, but instead of heading back to her beloved kitchen she sat still, and her eyes narrowed a touch. 'You knew it was Costa's wedding before the rest of us, didn't you?'

'I knew a little earlier,' Roula admitted, 'but I was told in confidence.'

'And you didn't think to share it with me?' Mia challenged. 'We're supposed to be best friends.'

'Let's not bring personal issues to work.'

'But you're the same out there.' Mia pointed beyond the retreat and her eyes were both hurt and angry. 'You never tell me anything any more. We shared everything growing up. God, Roula, your wedding was my first big event…'

'I know.'

'It's been five years since Dimitrios died!' Mia had stood up now, and was almost shouting. 'I've tried to be patient, but you keep shutting me out—'

'Mia,' Roula broke in. 'Not now.'

But there was no stopping Mia. 'Look, I'm not saying I understand what you're going through, but Dimitrios was my cousin and I loved him too. You used to talk to me, Roula…we used to share everything.'

No, not everything—and certainly not where her late husband was concerned.

Nobody knew Roula.

For, despite her bright smile at work and her

suitable widow persona in the village, at her very core Roula felt as if she had been annihilated. And her withdrawal from friendships, her slow self-annihilation, had taken place long before Dimitrios had died.

Roula had wanted to finish her studies, maybe study in Athens if she got the grades... But she had come home from school one day and been told she was to marry the popular and charismatic Dimitrios Drakos, who had his own fishing boat, and that his parents would gift them a cottage on the foreshore.

When Roula had cried her mother had come to speak with her. Pappa was ill—dying, in fact, she had told her. His dearest wish was to walk his daughter down the aisle. He had chosen wisely and wanted to be sure Roula was taken care of when he was gone.

She had been so naïve, so innocent, she hadn't even known the questions to ask.

Once a week to keep him happy.

That had been the full sum of her sex education.

So Roula had lain there on their wedding night as Dimitrios snored. She'd listened to the waves, but they had not soothed her, for she'd felt shocked, sore and ill. Not even the sound of birds greeting the dawn had brought comfort.

The only consolation Roula had had was that it

was done for another week... But then Dimitrios had stirred, rolled over, lifted her nightdress and done it again before he headed off night-fishing.

And again on his return.

Again and again and again...

No, Mia didn't need to know that about her cousin.

'Mia, I really don't think this is the time or place to be discussing our private lives...'

'There's *never* a good time with you, Roula,' Mia retorted, and went to flounce off. But she saved her parting shot for the office door. 'Since Dimitrios died it's as if I don't know you any more.'

Breathe out, Roula, she told herself. *And in.*

Roula buried her head in her hands and told herself that she would get through this and that she had survived much worse. Calming, she picked up the little glass frame on her desk and read the passage she loved so much. For despite everything, even if she'd questioned it and challenged it at times, Roula had clung on to her faith.

And I will restore to you the years that the locusts have taken.
Joel 2:25

And God had. Now she had peace in her life, and a career that she loved. And yet as she dragged in air Roula could almost feel the life she had rebuilt being snatched away...

For there was *another* secret.

One that would, by Roula's own doing, soon be getting out.

Her world was about to crumble, and here on the island only the bride and groom knew.

The bride wore...

Well, although she was dying to know, Roula hadn't had a chance to see yet. The bridal party had been whisked from the church straight to the private function. Roula had been busy with the beach party preparations as the meal was served.

Now, though, she might finally get a glimpse.

Roula stood out of sight in the archway of the minor function room, waiting to liaise with Beatrice. It was minor only in size, and perfect for intimate parties. It had been built around the remains of an ancient pillar and archway. She and Mia had used to play hide and seek on this very spot. The room was mainly windows, allowing nature to star and taking advantage of near-panoramic sea views. Right now, they were tinted a little, to avoid the afternoon glare of the sun, but tonight—weather allowing—the room would be bathed in stars.

'Fifteen minutes or so,' a waiter whispered. 'The *koumbaros* is just wrapping up.'

And then Roula heard a voice.

It wasn't necessarily a familiar voice, for it was very low, deep and measured, yet even if she couldn't see him, she knew unmistakably it was Galen.

'Well, I did warn Costa that I am the least suitable person for this role.'

Roula found that she wanted to move, to step out of the archway and glimpse her old friend.

Of course she couldn't step out, but she listened intently as he spoke.

'I am not good at jokes, nor am I sentimental, and neither do I share anecdotes...'

'The very reasons I didn't choose Leo,' Costa quipped, and the small gathering laughed.

Yes, Roula could well imagine Leo had plenty of colourful stories—it would seem Galen was indeed a wise choice.

'Mary...'

Roula heard Galen addressing the bride now, and lightly jesting with her.

'If you are feeling exasperated, please know that you are not alone. If you need someone to speak with, I'll completely understand. In truth, I have considered ending my friendship with Costa many times. A kitchen fire might not sound like a good reason,' Galen said. 'However, I was overseas and hadn't even spent a night in my new apartment. Nor was I aware it was being used for a New Year's Eve party...'

Roula smiled at the disgruntled edge to Galen's voice.

'Worse, though, was his attempt to paint over the fire damage. When you are back from your honeymoon I invite you to see what I mean.'

His serious tone had everyone really laughing, and Roula smiled again, because this intimate crowd would know that Galen was serious indeed—that brilliant mind let nothing go. He was affronted, only nicely so.

'Still,' Galen continued, 'each time I consider calling it a day I am forced to reflect—and, really, a more loyal, annoying, generous, exasperating...'

She didn't get to hear the rest as Beatrice had made her way over. 'Yolanda's starting to struggle. She's asked if you can make up a bed...'

'Sure.' Roula nodded, for she needed no further explanation. Yolanda had MS, and the sudden wedding would be taking its toll, though she would never let it show. It would be wise that she rest during the lull in proceedings before the beach party.

Roula left then, and by the time Yolanda arrived there was a bed in the area between the offices—a space big enough to accommodate both the bed and her electric wheelchair.

'Rest…' Roula said as she quietly shut the door to the offices, and then winced as the receptionist called to her.

'The Bridal Suite wants absinthe!'

'Shh…' Roula hushed her, because Stephanie could be rather loud. 'They have it.' Roula knew that because she had placed it there herself. 'You do mean the Bridal Suite—*not* the bridal party?'

'Leo Arati.'

'I'll call him,' Roula said, and promptly did so from her office, pulling his details up on the computer.

'Roula!' Leo greeted her warmly. 'You remembered!'

Sure enough, he had just found it. She snapped off more chocolate, for there had been no time for lunch or a break.

'What's absinthe?' Stephanie asked as she took another incoming call from a guest.

'Nobody can remember!' Roula laughed at her own joke, but then stopped smiling as the one problem she hadn't anticipated arrived.

'Temple Suite.' Stephanie replaced the phone and rolled her eyes. '*Not* happy!'

'Did he say why?'

'Not to lowly me—he wants management *now*! I said the guest services manager would be over shortly…'

That didn't sound like the Galen she had known.

Still, because it was her job to anticipate, Roula hazarded a guess as to what might be upsetting a tech wizard. She took a black bag from her drawer, then made her way over. And, yes, she was curious, as with bittersweet chocolate still melting on her tongue her mind wandered back to long-ago bittersweet days…

Oh, how she'd hated school when she'd first started.

Hated it!

The noise, the teasing about her red hair, the games she hadn't been invited to join... It had been too big, too scary, and Roula had started to wet her knickers.

Mortifying.

It had first happened in assembly, in front of the entire school.

Then again in her class.

Her peers had laughed and squealed, and she'd been scolded by her teacher and sent to change. A tall lady had wrapped her wet knickers into a paper parcel and told her off again.

'Roula Kyrios, this has to stop!'

She had wanted it to stop.

Roula had been placing the parcel in the bag on her peg, embarrassed to go back inside the classroom, when tears had threatened.

The other children would tease her more for that, Roula had known. She'd taken a breath and bunched her fists, and had been looking to the sky, fighting not to cry, when she'd heard his voice.

'It will all be okay.'

She'd jumped, because she had thought she was in the corridor alone, but it seemed Galen Pallas had been sent out of class.

'I don't want to go back in,' she'd admitted.

'I know.' He'd nodded. 'But you are brave.'

'I'm not.'

'Well, I think you are.'

And because the cleverest boy in the school had considered her brave, it had kind of made her so. At least enough to head back into class. Enough that a couple of years later, when he had again been beaten up and his lunch tossed away, Roula had left her little group and gone over to him, offered to share her lunch.

'No!' Galen had said sharply, without looking up. He'd been sitting on the grass, his knees pulled up, his head down as he'd plucked at the grass. But then he had added, 'Thank you, though.'

'Please,' Roula had said. 'I hate fig jam.' She hadn't—it had been her complete favourite.

'Go and join your friends or they'll tease you for speaking to me.'

'I don't care if they tease me. I'm sorry for what Nemo did to you.'

Galen had looked up. His eye had been swollen, his lip bloodied, and she had known that was why he'd been looking down when she had first spoken to him.

'It's not just your brother.'

'No...'

After that, every now and then, they would share her lunch.

By then Roula had always asked her mother for fig jam on her bread. Galen would help her with her maths problems and let her practise her English, which Roula was good at, though she'd struggled in art and maths.

Of course he'd got older, and so too had she. Roula had become popular, and best friends for ever with Mia, and had started to skip and hopscotch her way confidently through playtimes.

And then it had seemed as if she'd looked around one day to find that Galen was gone. He hadn't even said goodbye....

And now he was back.

Roula put her smile firmly in place and then knocked on the door.

She was met with familiar hazel eyes —but that was the only thing familiar.

Galen had not just grown from the lanky awkward youth she had last seen, he was very tall and although slim, somehow broad. His hair had always been clipped, but now it was worn longer and thicker, glossy and raven-black. Gone were the scruffy homemade clothes, and he was polished and elegant in his wedding suit.

Her breath hitched—for of course he would look different all these years on. But this new Galen, the thirty-something one, had hit her with an impact she had neither expected nor anticipated.

He was beautiful—and Roula had never contemplated male beauty before.

Ever.

Not even once.

He was standing there, phone in hand, dressed in a dark suit with a sprig of flowers in the lapel, a white shirt and silver tie. And, most noticeably, he was no longer awkward.

The awkward one was Roula, but she refused to acknowledge it, even to herself!

'Sir, I'm...'

'The guest services manager...' Galen finished for her as he looked at her badge.

He was doing his level best to hold on to his patience, but name badges irritated Galen. Always had. Especially when the person wearing one introduced herself with the title on the badge... Especially when he'd already been told that the guest services manager would be with him shortly...

He took a breath, aware that he was not, despite smiling since the crack of dawn, having the best day. But then he really saw the name, and he looked up and met dark brown eyes and— Who could forget that hair?

'Roula?'

'Yes,' she said. 'The guest ser...'

'Roula Kyrios?'

'Well, it's Drakos now.'

'Really?' Okay, not the best first response. Congratulations might have been better. But Galen didn't correct himself.

Married? Well, of course she would be, living here. And Dimitrios... He cast his mind back. Well, Galen hadn't moved in his circles, but he remembered him as good-looking and popular. As for Roula—well, she was seriously beau—

Galen abruptly halted his own thought process with a glance at her wedding ring.

'How can I help?' she asked.

Oh, yes, the Internet... Except this was *Roula*!

'So you're the guest serv...?' God, he was going to say those dreaded words again. He stopped himself. 'Still living here?'

'I am.' She smiled patiently. 'I was told that you wanted to speak to management.'

'Yes—I'm having trouble getting online. I can't even make a call.'

'There's no signal here. No internet either...'

'Excuse me?' He flashed her an incredulous smile.

'It's a health retreat. People come her for a digital detox—well, for many different types of detox, actually, but—'

'No, no,' Galen cut in. 'I'm not here to detox. I'm here for a wedding. A wedding I only found out about on Thursday night.'

'Yes.' Roula nodded. 'I thought it might prove an issue, and that is why I brought over the satellite phone…'

She held out a black bag and he took it and peered at the brick inside.

Good grief!

He took a very deep breath before attempting to explain the priority this was. 'There is an announcement soon to be made and I need to be online for it. I have one hour before I have to head out to the beach and plaster this grin on again…'

'I'm aware of the schedule, sir.'

He tried another angle. 'I bet Costa's villa has Internet access. I can guarantee it…'

'You would have to discuss that with him. There are guest-to-guest calls, of course…'

'Good,' he clipped, and went to stalk off. 'I'll do that now!'

'Yes,' Roula said. 'Why don't you call the groom and his new bride and ask to drop in on them? I'm sure Costa would be delighted to help you resolve this urgent matter.'

That stopped him, but not for long as he pondered how long a post-wedding bonk might take. 'How long do you think they'll…?'

Roula halted his inappropriate question with the tiniest raise of her brows—it was a tactic she occasionally used with difficult guests and, sadly, Galen was fast becoming one.

'Roula,' he said very patiently, 'I *know* that the Internet can be turned on.'

'It can't.'

She shook her head and he watched as a long titian curl sprung forward and freed itself from its confines, like some old-fashioned jack-in-the-box. *Surprise!* And, like those old-fashioned boxes, the spring did not straighten out, and nor did it jump back. It draped, amber, gold and spent, across her cheek. Galen wanted to reach for her hair…he would like to pop that curl back, to tuck it in, and then for it to surprise him all over again.

'Pardon?' Galen said, because while watching her hair he had lost track of her words.

'I said, even if you were the King of England, I could not give you a signal or Internet access. What I *can* do is give you the use of my office once the bridal party has moved down to the beach.'

'How about now?'

'I'm sorry.' She shook her head, loose curl and all. 'I'm sure you understand that the smooth running of the wedding has to remain my priority.'

He stood silent.

'Is there anything else I can help you with?' she asked.

'Actually, yes. Didn't you get the brief from my PA?'

'The brief?' she frowned. 'Regarding...?'

'Bed linen.' Galen said. 'I prefer plain.'

Roula looked past the columns to the sleeping chambers. The Temple Suite was beyond anything she had ever seen, and the very best of the luxurious retreat. It had its own vast internal pool, and beneath an incredible dome was a bed so high it looked like an altar—and it was dressed in the bespoke Temple Suite bedding: a pale velvet with a *very* subtle hand-embroidered star constellation.

And he was complaining!

'I don't believe I did get that.' Roula gave a tight smile, trying to be diplomatic because she didn't want his PA to be in trouble, but, no, of *course* she hadn't got a brief! 'I believe Costa arranged all the bookings.'

'But I specifically messaged Kristina...'

'I apologise for the oversight.'

Oh, Galen, Roula thought, her smile fading as she let herself out. *How you've changed.*

CHAPTER THREE

IT WAS A minor glitch.

So very minor in the scheme of things.

Mia was hyperventilating as the chefs from Santorini commandeered her kitchen. Yolanda had been difficult to wake up, and so tired she'd actually needed a little help from Roula into her chair. And Leo Arati had had to be gently prompted, several times, and told that it was time to head to the beach for the party.

There were just a million balls, but Roula was actually very used to juggling them at work.

She stood, her work smile on, as the party took off. All were invited. The chefs, waiters and security guards were all externally hired, and rarely the retreat was running on a skeleton staff for a few hours.

Beatrice and Roula were the skeletons!

'Aunty Roula!' Dimitrios's twin nieces came running towards her, all dark curls and huge brown eyes, the sweetest girls on earth.

'There's going to be dress-up soon!' the leader of the two declared.

'But you're already dressed up!' Roula teased, for she knew what they meant. Soon the music would start, and there was a dressing up area and a photo booth for all the children, and *of course* the twins knew it. 'You both look beautiful.'

'But they're starting to give numbers out…'

'Are they?'

'We're going to be last.'

Roula smiled and then put her hand in her pocket and took out two numbered tokens. 'Shh…'

'Will we be first?'

'No,' Roula said, 'that would not be fair.' She gave them a tiny wink. 'But you will be third and fourth!'

They were the sweetest, cheekiest pair, and she waved to their father as the little ones scampered off. Stephanos, Dimitrios's brother-in-law, waved back, and then helped the baby he was carrying wave too.

Roula smiled, but then blew out a breath. Her confrontation with Mia had shaken her, perhaps? Or was it her knowledge of the news to come? Would she see still be able to see the twins? Roula had held them the day they were born…

It fully dawned on her then that her time here might be ending. That her family, her home, her career were silently coming undone—the truth, when revealed, would *not* be setting her free.

Galen wasn't faring so well either.

In dutiful *koumbara* mode he worked the beach.

He loathed mingling and small talk at the best of times, but he kept his smile on and made dreaded chit-chat. Yet his eyes kept drifting.

There was no doubt the retreat was marvellous, but it was the village in the distance he scanned. There was the church where he had stood silently as his *yaya* had openly wept each week. He looked upwards at the lush hilly terrain, at the winding road that hugged steep slopes and had claimed his parents and almost him.

'You must see a lot of changes…?' someone said.

'No,' Galen responded, and saw the startlement of the small group nearby. 'Well, of course the retreat is incredible. I meant the village looks the same…'

'But it's completely different,' one of the man insisted. 'Designer shops now, cafés and restaurants, a medical centre…'

'Of course,' Galen agreed, choosing not to explain that he had meant the skyline, and the roads carved into his brain so clearly he could almost see the school bus heaving it slow way up the hill.

'Some familiar faces…?'

'Yes,' Galen said. 'Your father was the postmaster…'

'Still is.' The man nodded. 'Well, he retires soon. Hey, Pa…' He called the elderly man over. 'Remember Galen?'

Again his gaze drifted, though now it swept the beach. On the edge of the activities stood Roula, talking and laughing with two little girls who were identical twins.

'Who else have you caught up with?' the post-master asked.

Galen had the memory of an elephant—except when it came to irrelevant names.

'Yolanda, of course...' Galen said. 'And Mia...' He had never really liked Mia, but today he was *koumbara*, Galen reminded himself. 'The wedding lunch was excellent...' Galen smiled politely, even though he felt the gnaw of indigestion.

'Poor Roula...' One of the women followed his gaze. 'We were just saying how hard today must be for her...' She sighed dramatically. '*She* was promised to Costa...'

Galen almost laughed in her face—and not pleasantly. Roula would have barely been at school when that ridiculous promise had been made. But the money-hungry Kyrios family had changed their mind when Yolanda had fallen ill and her husband had left her. Bastards.

Still, it was not Galen who disputed the observation.

'No...' the old postmaster corrected. 'I told you—Roula misses Dimitrios.' He must have seen Galen's frown. 'You didn't know?'

It was then that he found out that Roula had been widowed.

'So sad…they were so happy. You know…' the postmaster leant in a little closer to Galen '…five years on and she still sleeps on the couch.' He tapped his nose. 'I deliver parcels. She tries not to let me see in…'

'Excuse me, please.' Galen pushed out his plastic smile. God, but he loathed this place and the gossipmongers—like hyenas with a carcass. And he fed himself into another group, but the conversation was much the same.

The bride was too thin…a little too clingy.

Oh, she'd done *very* well for herself.

And Roula was one of the topics too.

Her career was all she had.

Such a shame they'd never had babies.

Galen hated this place.

There were, though, some friendly faces.

'God!' Leo gave a dramatic sigh when they caught up with each other. 'Kill me now.'

'Good to be back?' Galen grinned.

'I absolutely adore coming to the retreat,' Leo admitted, 'but there you're rather shielded from the locals and my ghastly family. How are you faring, Galen?'

'It's a good wedding,' Galen said, because he just didn't bitch—even with friends. And, of course, some people were lovely. But it was the maliciousness behind certain smiles that rankled. The opinions so readily voiced.

He glanced over towards Roula and found that he was frowning.

He watched her look up to the sky and saw her shoulders lift, and he remembered that day—gosh, years ago…decades, perhaps—when she'd stood at her peg and wept. He saw her hands clench and he was certain now that she was about to break down…

Not here, Roula, he silently urged.

There were already enough poisoned arrows flying around. He could just imagine how the locals would feast on it if she cried. And even before that thought had been processed Galen left his friend and walked towards her.

'You said you could get me a connection.'

'Sorry?'

Roula was startled. Her eyes were brimming, and Galen knew he had been right. She was on the very edge of tears and needed to get the hell away from here.

Now.

'I need to get online,' he snapped. 'So either you get me to an internet connection now, or you find someone who can…'

'Of course.' She gestured towards the main offices. 'This way, please.'

They came into an empty reception area and

she took him behind the desk, then gestured to her own office. Galen pretended not to notice her glassy brown eyes and the pink tip of her nose.

'Please,' Roula said. 'Help yourself.'

'Thank you.'

Galen took a seat and looked not at the computer but at the endless items that crowded her desk. The chocolate he understood, but there were photos, quotes, flowers, rosary beads... There was even a little dragonfly stuck to her computer screen. Galen was untidy himself, though his desk was cluttered with coffee cups and food, not endless pictures of grinning twins staring back at him. How the hell did she work in this riot?

'Galen?' Roula knocked, but stood outside the door. Unlike the postmaster, she made no attempt to peer in. 'I apologise—you will need my password.'

'It's fine. I'm already in.'

'But I didn't give it to you...'

'Easy guess,' Galen said. 'You really need something more secure.'

He grimaced when he saw the dip in charts his absence had caused, but then flicked off the page, and called the care home to find out how the new treatment regime that had been arranged before he'd flown off was faring. Yaya was on her second unit of blood, he was told, but had twice removed the IV.

'She has one-on-one care, though?' Galen checked, because it had been agreed she would while she was receiving treatment.

'Of course—but she is quick.'

'Very quick for ninety,' Galen said. 'One-on-one care,' he reminded them, and then dropped the phone.

Despite the rather rich lunch, he ate some of Roula's chocolate. He was annoyed with the carers and glad for a brief respite in a long, long day, with the private after-party still to come.

Roula also wished the day was over.

She looked at the sky as the blazing sun dipped down and could already feel the throb of music from the beach. Thankfully she had composed herself by the time Galen reappeared, and she looked up and smiled.

'Did you see the announcement?' Roula asked as she stood up.

'Sorry?'

'The one you needed the Internet for?'

'Oh, that.' He gave those hazel eyes a little roll. 'I was supposed to be making the announcement. Well, my foundation. But...'

Roula gulped. 'Did it cause problems? The delay...?'

'The price has crashed, but that happens a lot in crypto... It will recover.' He considered for a moment. 'Well, maybe.'

Oh, no! She should have woken Yolanda earlier, got this man to a connection... 'I'm so sorry.'

'Roula, don't worry about it.'

He gave her a smile then, and possibly it was the scent from the candles—only they weren't lit yet—but she breathed in something beautiful, something soothing, just a moment of calm...

And Roula felt something she had not felt for so long now.

Normal.

CHAPTER FOUR

THE BEACH PARTY was over.

Finally!

Roula's heels were about to come off for the final time as she updated the overnight team. 'The beach is almost cleared,' Roula said. 'The private party will go for ages, but I'm out of here.'

'Not yet, you're not.' Stephanie halted her. 'Costa's just asked if you could bring some more cake. Mia is just slicing it.'

'Can't someone else do that?' Roula groaned. She was honestly exhausted—but then she stirred herself. Mia had already been invited for a drink, Beatrice too. It was just Costa being polite with the senior staff. 'Of course I'll go.'

'Here.' Mia handed her the tray she had prepared but did not meet Roula's eyes.

'Thank you,' Roula said. 'I've heard from the guests that lunch was amazing...seriously so.'

Mia said nothing in return.

Roula carried the tray in—of course with a smile. It really was a small gathering. Yolanda had retired and it was just the happy couple, along with Galen, Leo and Deacon, and a few people who were, she guessed, Athens friends.

'Roula!' Costa looked up. 'You're off duty now.'

'Soon.' She kept her *no problem* smile on.

'I meant join us,' Costa said. 'Please. Relax.'

'Thank you, though not for long—'

'Roula,' Costa interrupted. 'You're staying.'

'Old friends,' Leo chimed in. 'Gosh, how long since we've all been together?'

'Leo, I see you all the time.' Roula smiled.

'I meant us four.'

Roula didn't answer.

They were soon back to whatever they'd been discussing before Roula had arrived.

'She was awful to Mary,' Costa said, and then politely brought Roula up to speed. 'We're discussing Galen's PA. I had to bribe her with a babymoon just to get her to pick up Mary from the airport. You could not meet a colder woman.'

But Galen shrugged. 'Kristina is not employed to pick up your girlfriends from the airport, Costa...'

'Fair enough,' Costa conceded. 'Though she's not exactly looking out for you either.'

'Rubbish,' Leo interjected. 'She's devoted.'

'No, I work in the same building,' Costa insisted, 'Kristina wouldn't notice if he was dead at his desk...'

It was light-hearted banter, really, and Roula actually slipped off her shoes as she sipped her champagne.

'I'm serious,' Costa continued. 'Once Kristina left him in the office on a Friday, after he'd already been there all day. She came back on Monday and didn't even look in on him...'

'I'm not an infant,' Galen said. 'I had said I was not to be disturbed. I wanted to focus.'

'He collapsed when he came out,' Costa informed the people at the table, and they all laughed. 'Dehydrated. All that brain and he forgot about H_2O.'

'I got a hell of a lot done though...' Galen shrugged and took a drink of his iced tea.

'I know Kristina's married and everything...' Leo pressed on. 'Due to have a baby soon?'

'Correct,' Galen nodded. 'She's in her third trimester.'

Roula felt a little uncomfortable now—just as she had when they were at school and the boys would tease Galen and he'd never realise until too late that they were...

'It's the million-dollar question, really.' Leo sighed dramatically. 'Come on, Galen, we're just dying to know. Were you two ever, or are you still—?'

'Leo,' Galen cut in, and his voice was calm but there was the sharp edge of warning. 'I would never discuss one of my staff's personal life—not with them, and most certainly not with you.'

'Ooh!' Leo beamed as he was duly told off. 'Well, you can't blame me for trying to find out.'

Unfazed, he turned his gossipy smile to Roula. 'How was your day, dear Roula?'

'Busy!'

'Do the locals all still think you're upset over him?' Leo asked, and gestured with his head towards Costa, who laughed.

'Some do.' Roula nodded. 'You know what they can be like here.'

Leo sighed. 'This place! Can't they accept you might just be grieving your husband?'

Galen noted Roula's brief grim smile and then he looked away.

Five years since her husband had died and yet it was spoken about as if it was a recent event.

Still, time did not move on readily here—and neither did widows... Galen knew very well the rules of this place. Just as his *yaya* had, Roula would attend church for all souls on a Saturday, as well as go on Sunday, and then there'd be his annual memorial...

Where, he wondered, did beautiful widows go for relief? And Roula was undeniably beautiful...

It didn't enter his head that she might not have such requirements, because he so often did. It was necessary. Like food, like water...

Admittedly, he forgot to eat or drink on occasion, as had been outlined tonight by his friends. But after famine came feast...

He considered her options and found there were not many—for there was no chance of her taking a discreet lover in Anapliró that Galen could see.

So where do you go, Roula?

Did she take the ferry to Santorini and meet a lover? Galen was quietly turned on at that thought of her leaving it all behind for a steamy afternoon. Or maybe an occasional stolen sultry Santorini night, before returning to Anapliró as if butter wouldn't melt...

He liked that thought.

Galen remained seated when the others decided to go around popping balloons—there had apparently been a specification from Costa that there were many.

Roula, it would seem, was not a popping balloons type of person either, for now it was just the two of them at the lavish table, and Roula was fiddling with a plaster on her thumb.

'Did you enjoy the day?' Roula asked politely. 'The beach party...?' Her voice trailed off as clearly she recalled the internet issues he'd raised. She moved to safer ground. 'Everyone said the meal was beautiful.'

'It was a bit too rich for me,' Galen said.

He was just being honest—his guts had been burning since lunch and usually he had the constitution of an ox. Galen watched her lips, parted ready to jump in and defend her friend Mia, but then she pushed out her work smile.

'The guest is always right, Roula.' He was gently provoking her, and with specific intent. 'Isn't that so?'

'Of course,' Roula responded politely.

Galen waited silently for the real Roula to be revealed—for the fiery person he'd known to fire back a tart retort. Yet it never came.

'How is Kupia Florakis?' she asked, about his *yaya*. 'She's in Athens, yes?'

'Doing well for ninety.' He nodded. 'She misses here.'

'Will you go up to the house?' Roula asked. 'Perhaps take something back for her?'

'It was all very last minute. I was only told about the wedding on Thursday night.'

'We didn't find out much before that,' Roula admitted, glancing up as a couple who were topping up their drinks in between balloon-popping chimed into their conversation.

'Nor us—we were taking bets about your plus one, Galen.'

'Not a chance,' Galen said.

'Told you!' The woman smiled at her partner. 'I said he'd be here on his own.'

'Have you just broken up with someone?' Roula asked.

'No.' He shook his head. 'Nothing to break.'

'Oh, sorry. I thought when they said they were taking bets...'

'They were being facetious.'

'About you being single?'

'I don't date,' Galen said. 'Believe me, the thought of a long weekend entertaining some-one...' He shook his head. 'No.'

'"Entertaining"?' Roula checked.

'Breakfast, flying together, driving to the air-port, getting ready...' He must have seen her frown. 'I don't do well with relationships.'

'Well, I'm sure you'll...'

Roula looked, and then looked again. Because even if she was dead inside—well, there was no denying Galen was stunning.

'I'm sure the right person is out there.'

'Roula,' he said, and looked directly at her. 'I think we may have crossed wires—I actively *choose* not be in a relationship.'

'Oh...' Roula said, relieved they had found a common thread. 'Like me.'

For the first time that evening their eyes met.

Galen didn't flirt—there was no need when he were as beautiful as he was—but, more than that, romance was not an arena he played in. His refusal to acknowledge her entrance to the party had been...well, deliberate. For he was skilled at a certain game. He was also discerning and discreet.

And he chose his moment now, when the rest were distracted, and offered invitation with his eyes.

If Roula was interested he was about to find out, for she now glanced towards him and met his gaze.

Her eyes were brown—that he already knew—and yet for the first time Galen ventured into their burnt umber.

Where do you go, Roula? he asked silently, and when she did not look away his hazel gaze delved a little further. *Do you want to go there with me?*

Roula found herself caught in his line of vision and for a brief moment had the sensation of being pulled by a gentle undertow—floating mindlessly, willingly, as the noise of the revellers around them seemed to dim.

It was the oddest sensation—to be locked in another's eyes—but perhaps only because she'd never been asked if she'd like to indulge before, had only ever been taken, Roula misread the question.

Was he still cross about earlier? she wondered. Because she felt a little... She wasn't sure what. Anxious, perhaps...scrutinised, maybe?

Roula flicked her gaze away.

'Hey, Galen…' someone called.

A little bewildered, Roula stood. 'Excuse me.'

'You're going?' he checked, and she saw that he wore just a smudge of a frown.

'Not yet.'

Roula was warm, and also a little flustered as she briefly escaped to the bathroom. She did what she had to and then, washing her hands, decided to top up her lipstick.

It was a party after all.

Yet even as she added a slick of coral she was still replaying that moment with Galen and trying to interpret it into a language she knew. Perhaps he didn't appreciate staff mingling with the guests? Or was he still irritated that she hadn't been able to get him online…

Her thoughts stopped as the door opened. 'Mary!' She turned as the bride came in. 'You look completely beautiful.' Roula was actually in awe of the fact that a bride could still look so gorgeous after midnight. The formal dress had been replaced by the slip version which she had worn earlier on the beach, and her blonde hair tumbled. 'Stunning.'

'Just happy.' Mary smiled. 'I never dreamt we'd be having the actual wedding service in London…' Her eyes brimmed with tears. 'Did you know?'

'There were *many* back-up plans,' Roula told her. 'I am so glad it all came together.'

'I just wasn't expecting my dad to be there. Yolanda too, and Galen...' She gave a low, devilish laugh. 'Mind you, apparently Costa thought he'd lost him at one point...'

'Lost him?'

'He was catching up with a *friend*, apparently.' Mary gave an exaggerated roll of her eyes. 'As you do at six a.m. on the morning of a wedding.'

'I'm not with you...'

'Galen was with one his catch-up girls.' Mary laughed again. 'It would seem that he has a very devoted fan base in every port!'

Roula's laugh came a little too late. She was so out of step with everything. She'd been thinking Galen was single, or even celibate, perhaps, when actually... Gosh! She replayed their conversation and realised it would seem that when it came to relationships, Galen cherry-picked the parts he wanted...

And they were the very parts Roula most certainly didn't!

'How are you doing?' Mary asked.

Roula dragged her mind back to more familiar terrain. 'Oh, it's been busy, but...'

'How are you holding up?'

Costa had no doubt asked Mary to corner her like this, to find out how she was faring. Roula had immediately known the reason for the rapid wedding—and, no, it wasn't as half the island was suggesting. Costa just wanted the woman he loved by his side and out of danger.

And, as Roula had recently found out, her older brother Nemo might be very dangerous indeed…

'Have you heard anything?' Mary asked anxiously.

'No.' Roula shook her head and then reminded Mary of what they'd been told. 'The police said not to discuss it.'

'Even so…'

'Mary.' Roula was practical. 'This is your wedding! Focus on enjoying it!' She refused to let anything spoil Mary's day. 'Get out there and have fun. Guest Service Manager's orders.'

'You're off duty,' Mary pointed out.

'Then *I* want to have some fun,' Roula lied, because in truth she just wanted to head for home.

Nobody knew Roula.

They returned to the table. Roula's smile was back in place, and she even took her jacket off and placed it over the chair, to denote that she was reluctantly—not that she showed it—staying.

She refilled her glass, but with water this time, and took a grateful refreshing drink. Galen was still there and, given Mary's recent revelation about him, she was embarrassed at her earlier reply.

Gosh, had Galen been flirting with her or coming on to her? Had he thought she was doing it back at him?

Yikes.

'Galen?' she said, and when he glanced over, she corrected her earlier response to his single status. *'Not* like me!'

To his credit, Galen gave her a very nice smile. 'Pity.'

Roula almost laughed. Gosh, he'd certainly been barking up the wrong tree with her. And now, very politely, he'd stopped barking.

Not that he had been really, but... Well, there were no more undercurrents, no stolen looks— just the last moments of a gorgeous wedding.

And of course Roula had work the next day...

'I'm going to head off,' she whispered to Leo.

'Don't you dare,' Leo said as she attempted to depart discreetly. 'Stay and hear my speech at least...'

'Leo, no.' Galen was assertive, but he combined it with humour as he stood and averted disaster—because Leo was less than discreet. 'You are *not* stealing my thunder—I give the best man speeches.'

To everyone's relief he took to the microphone and his speech was very concise.

'Mary and Costa: *ee ora ee kale!*' Galen offered his best wishes for perhaps the twentieth time that day. 'The time is good,' he said, and then he added, 'Now we dance.'

Oh, they danced!

Well, not Galen. He remained seated and Roula wondered if she could slip away. Mary and Costa were draped around each other as Leo, deprived of the microphone, played DJ, and the others joined them.

'Come on, you two!' they urged, begging them to join in, and he looked over to Roula.

'We're killjoys,' Roula said.

'I always am.' Galen nodded. 'I hate dancing—I find it pointless.'

Roula found that she was smiling, and they shared an eye-roll as they were summoned again.

'Shall we?' he offered.

Whatever the silent conversation they'd briefly engaged in had meant had long since been dropped, and for old times' sake she smiled. 'One dance,' Roula said, 'then I'm really going to go…'

He held one of her hands up, as if they were in a half-formal dance, and felt her fingers cold beneath his. The other was light on her bare upper arm.

It was a polite dance.

Galen *was* polite.

Always.

At least out of the bedroom…

But he only played with the very willing, and Roula had made it clear that she wasn't, so he'd ended the game back at the table.

His grip did not tighten, and nor did he touch her hair, which was uncoiling down her back. It was a dance with a long-ago friend.

Pointless.

Two people standing fully dressed and moving, but going nowhere.

And this was a particularly wooden dance—or rather one with a porcelain figurine. For she was rigid in his arms and held herself back from him.

'I ate the chocolate on your desk,' Galen said.

'I know you did.' Roula nodded. 'How did you know my password?'

'I'm good at retaining numbers. Your date of birth,' Galen said. 'And your little dog Benji...'

She gave a soft laugh. 'I still miss him.'

Perhaps dancing wasn't quite so pointless.

Her hair smelt like sunshine, and her once cold hand had warmed to match the temperature of his, and the almost imperceptible beginnings of a thaw was taking place in his arms. Not much... just the dusting of her curls on his chin as she moved a little more freely...yet it felt so rewarding.

They were polar opposites.

Roula was a nice Anapliró girl, and that generally meant commitment before bed—or at the very least dinners and conversation and all the things he just did not do. Though he would like to stroke the skin on her arms beneath his fingers. Just to feel the shiver that was, he was almost sure, there between them.

Not acknowledged.

Not quite…

Roula felt his shift in awareness and could not quantify it, for they were dancing the same dance and he held her the same way. Yet his scent made her want to breathe deeper. And from nothing of note she felt a band of constriction from the two bras which she always wore to flatten her generous breasts.

It was just a moment during a dance, but what had felt simply natural suddenly flustered her as the moment—whatever it was—dispersed.

'Are you okay?' Galen asked.

Roula frowned, for it was as if he had felt her sudden tension. 'Of course.'

Yet she wasn't. It really was time to go home. But she was saved from making an excuse to leave, because the music suddenly died and they both looked over at the sound of a crash.

Leo had faded rather abruptly!

It was quite fun, watching Deacon carry him out, and then Mary and Costa were cheered and clapped off to bed, and like soapy bubbles the little crowd started to disperse.

'It was nice to see you again,' Roula said.

'And you,' Galen agreed. 'Roula, I heard about…' He faltered. 'Well, I'm sorry—'

'Please…' she rapidly cut in, and then corrected herself. 'You weren't to know.'

'How many years *has* it been?' Galen asked, and he was not discussing her late husband. 'I mean since we saw each other?'

'I'm not sure,' Roula said, but there was a slight edge to her voice as she spoke. 'You're the one who's good with numbers.'

He found himself staring into unblinking umber eyes and saw that there was turmoil there. Despite popular opinion on the island, Galen was not a robot—or *rompot* as he'd been called in Greek.

'Are you…?' He didn't know how to ask if she missed her husband. 'Weddings must be hard.'

'There's one every week here.'

'I meant—'

'Please don't try to guess about me, Galen. It's the national sport here.'

Galen looked at her then, at that gorgeous hair in the moonlight, stripped of colour, and her face so pale. It felt surreal to be here. To stand in a place so familiar, with someone he'd once known and yet no longer recognised.

He thought of her near tears on the beach—not

that she was aware he knew she'd almost cried. But she was hurting today. Galen was sure.

And so he broke the heavy silence.

'Anonymous conversation helps sometimes, I believe...' he said.

'You're not anonymous, Galen.'

'Sort of...' he said.

'No, thank you,' Roula said, and then rather tartly added, 'To both offers.'

Galen knew exactly to what she was referring—for, yes, there had been two offers made tonight.

Roula pushed out her best guest services manager smile. 'I hope the remainder of your stay is a pleasant one.'

'Roula...?'

'Goodnight, Galen.'

Roula slipped away into the dark of the night. She could hear the roar of the sea and feel the whip of wind on her cheeks, and she was hurting and confused and so cross, so furious, that she felt like screaming.

Instead she walked faster, almost at a run.

Mia had upset her, Roula told herself as she marched along dark familiar streets. And Mia was wrong. They had grown apart long before Dimitrios's death.

She had tried to broach her issues once, at a

girls' lunch. Ella, his sister, had been pregnant with the twins, and had told them that Stephanos wanted to get the snip, so they could 'do it' worry-free.

They had all laughed.

Her face burning, Roula had broached the subject, desperate for some advice. 'Dimitrios wants it all the time...'

'Newlyweds!' Ella had smiled. 'We never came up for air. But wait till you have kids...'

'Young love...' Mia had sighed. 'I'm jealous— the only thing keeping me up at night is meal prep!'

Roula had come away even more confused, and had never so much as hinted at her private hell again.

Never.

Even when it had got worse.

The lunches with friends had stopped. The sex and violence had not. There had been no babies, and that was all her fault, and each month his rage had increased.

Her retreat had started.

'I might apply for work as a chambermaid,' she had said one day as she'd put down his dinner, nervous to admit to him that she had already put in her application.

'Why would you work for Costa Leventis?'

Dimitrios had stood up from the table. 'You wish you'd married him, don't you?'

'Of course not. Dimitrios, please...'

'Why would you want to work for him when I'm working night after night to provide for you?'

To say they'd 'made love' would not be the term she would have used even in her most naïve times.

To say they'd 'had sex' did not suffice either...

Roula was crying as she let herself into her little fisherman's cottage, the flashes of memory too much. All she had held in during this long, dreadful day burst like a dam as she went through the door—only to be greeted by her wedding photo.

'Damn you!' she said, and took off her wedding ring and placed it on the mantelpiece, then turned down the photo as she always did when she was home alone.

Roula headed into the bedroom to retrieve her bed linen from the wardrobe. Usually she did not so much as glance at the marital bed as she passed it, but tonight—or rather early this morning—she glared at it.

The coastguard had come to her door in the middle of the night to say Dimitrios's boat had been spotted ablaze, and as his family had arrived she had dashed to the bedroom to get dressed.

Dressed in whatever one wore wear when one's husband was missing at sea.

Get dressed, Roula, she'd told herself.

She had walked into the bedroom and closed the door. The sound of a helicopter had been loud overhead and the wail of the sirens urgent as she'd glanced at the bed.

A couple of her long red hairs had lain on the pillow. She usually picked them off and then turned the pillow over. But that morning her hand had reached out and then pulled back...

She'd heard the wailing and sobbing starting up outside as she'd stood there and stared at her marital bed.

Please God, she had silently begged, may I never have to set foot in that bed again.

And to this very day Roula slept on the couch.

CHAPTER FIVE

GALEN HEADED BACK to the Temple Suite, peeled off his suit and took a long drink of water.

It was icy cold and pure, and so instantly refreshing that he conceded there was one thing about Anapliró he missed.

Galen refilled the glass, took the sprig of flowers from his lapel and placed them into the water.

Duty had been fulfilled.

It was done.

Well, not quite.

He stripped off and got into the pool and lay on his back, liking the weightlessness, choosing not to reflect on the day.

It had been a disaster workwise.

Galen hauled himself out of the pool and lay on the now plain linen and looked up at the dome. He'd forgotten just how beautiful the stars were here. How, as a child, he would creep out at night just to stare up at the Milky Way and try to spot the stars he had read about.

Yaya had said he wandered.

No.

Sometimes…

But usually it was to sit or to lie and stare up, as he did now.

Galen found Scorpio easily and thought that

the stars above did not itch like the ones that had been on the bedlinen…they were soothing…

Roula must have thought him a right bastard, Galen thought. A demanding guest. Perhaps he was? But the guest services manager did not need to know of his issues with fabric, or the chaos missing his announcement had caused. Perhaps it was a good thing he couldn't get online now and see the charts!

Rarely, he wished for a moment to explain himself. He had long ago given up on doing that, but he would have liked to explain things better to Roula.

Galen took a breath, and to distract himself fixed his gaze on the star Antares. But there was no escape there, for with its reddish glow he thought of her hair uncoiling.

Roula Kyrios… With her fiery red hair she had once been so strong with her opinions, and with a laugh so infectious that he could recall it now.

Ha-ha, breath, ha-ha-ha, breath, ha-ha-ha-ha…

She hadn't laughed that way tonight.

Maybe your laugh changed after childhood? he considered.

Possibly.

Or perhaps it faded away when your husband died?

Where do you go to, Roula?

Galen decided he would not be going there!

Instead, he hauled himself from the bed. Hopefully Kristina had managed to brief his maid properly and his running gear would be there.

It was, so he dressed and put on his small running pack. Under a pre-dawn sky he took the familiar road up the hill towards his old home, but that was not his destination. It took ten, maybe fifteen minutes to get into rhythm, and then he made his way up the steep incline.

The last of the stars were fading in the sky when he first saw the *kandylakia* for his parents. The roadside shrines were dotted amongst all these hilly roads. Each different, some were like little houses, but his parents' shrine was a tiny replica of the village church where they had married and were now buried together. It was set high on a stone, near where the accident had occurred.

It was not the gradient Galen was tackling that had his throat hitching as he jerked in air—more that he could see a candle was lit inside it.

The locals had always taken care of these roadside memorials, but he had thought that by now... Or rather he had tried *not* to think about it standing neglected, like the house...

It had not been neglected.

He opened up the little door and took out a few

fading flowers. He put in the ones he had worn yesterday. There was a box of matches inside, and fresh candles.

He had always turned his head away as they'd passed it on the school bus. Today, he saw its beauty. And he wished he had faith, but he stuck to logic.

He looked around, examined the tree, and could barely locate the scar on it. His parents had died here, and the trajectory of his whole life had changed right at this spot.

It offended Galen's consciousness that he couldn't remember a thing about it. Nor could he remember the months in hospital afterwards.

And so, instead of standing there and trying to remember what he could not, Galen ran down towards the *theatron*, where he and Costa had used to train.

As Galen took the steps again, he recalled being small and running up and down, over and over. Preparing to face a day of being shoved. And then getting taller and wider and still running, because he'd thought his brain might explode if he stayed there much longer.

Yet one night here and he was already considering staying on for another...sorting out the house...just getting it done...

For things had been left undone.

Galen's run finished rather abruptly, and as he dragged in air he took a seat reluctantly. The silence was actually beautiful here on Anapliró. There was a haze of sea mist over the Aegean, softly fading into a clear blue sky, and it was a colour he could not describe. There was no hum of traffic, no lights or anything. It was like a power-cut, when all appliances stopped, and you realised the world you sat in was not so silent after all.

Maybe he did need that digital detox, Galen thought wryly, because his mind was actually feeling a new version of clear.

'Galen!'

He looked up when he heard his name being called, and then frowned when he saw that it was Costa. 'What the hell?' Galen asked. 'Haven't you got better things to do the morning after you marry?'

'I do—but I need to speak with you, and of course there was no chance to do so yesterday. I guessed I might find you here.'

They both sat on a damp, dewy step and Costa handed Galen some water. 'Are you and Mary the fastest break up ever?' he asked.

'No…' Costa was turning his own water bottle over and over in his hand, as he had the champagne cork. 'But I need to ask you to do something.'

'What? More speeches!'

'Kristina is taking six weeks off, yes?'

'What's that got to do with you?'

'I'm going to ask you to employ someone. You're going to say no, but I—'

'I'll save you the trouble,' Galen cut in. 'The answer is no. Stay out of my work!'

'Galen, I told you there was stuff going on.'

Galen turned at the gravity in Costa's tone.

'This is a serious matter...'

And Galen knew that it must be if the groom was here at seven in the morning the day after his wedding.

'Please just listen?'

Galen gave a reluctant nod.

'This can go no further—ever.'

'You know it won't.'

'You know that Roula and I were briefly promised to each other—'

'Oh, please,' Galen cut in. 'You were kids. Anyway, she married Golden Boy...'

'I know that, and so does Roula, but her brother Nemo—he's my head of security...'

'Another reason never to employ family or friends,' Galen said, because Nemo was a brute and had made his life hell.

'You're right,' Costa agreed. 'Because when I brought Mary here for the first time he tried to set her up as a thief. I now believe he wanted to break us up…'

Galen frowned at Costa's ominous tone.

'I tried to speak to Roula about it—she's been odd for weeks…'

'And?' Galen snapped, impatient for information now.

'On her birthday she found a gas cylinder hidden in her brother's garage. She recognised it from Dimitrios's boat.'

'She's sure?'

'Sure enough that she went to the police. They're taking it very seriously. It would seem there have been several suspicious transactions made by Nemo.'

'You're saying that Nemo killed Roula's husband to clear the way for her to marry you?'

'He hasn't been charged,' Costa said, and then added, 'Yet. But there's a lot of resentment there. Now that I'm rich, Roula's family are bitter that they pulled out of the arrangement.'

'She's not a piece of real estate.'

'Tell that to Nemo.'

Galen closed his eyes. *This place!*

'The Drakos family are going to kick off, and

her family too, when they find out that she was the one who informed on her brother—'

'I get it,' Galen cut in. No wonder Roula had been upset yesterday.

'If you offered Roula a temporary—'

'No.' Galen shut down Costa's solution straight away, for he did not bring his personal life to work in any way shape or form. 'Arrangements have already been put in place. But I've got the guest apartment. Tell her she's welcome to use that.'

'Roula can't know I've discussed this with you!' Exasperated, Costa waved a hand. 'Believe me, I have tried to help, but she says she has it all under control. Mary approached her last night, but she was quickly shut down...'

'Then maybe she *does* have it under control.'

'Galen,' Costa said. 'Roula was going to walk into the police station without a lawyer.'

Galen swore.

'Roula will only take the job if she thinks it's a genuine one.'

'Then I'll find her something...'

'Something!' Costa gave an incredulous laugh. 'Galen, she's very career-minded. Believe me, she's not going to leave here for some admin role in one of your offsite offices, but a temporary

PA position for Galen Pallas would look good on her CV...'

'I don't like this, Costa.'

On so many levels Galen did not like it—he did not want his worlds colliding, and he chose his staff carefully. He loathed emotion and drama— the very things this island thrived on.

There was another issue too, but he pushed that out of his mind for now. Instead, he thought of a day long ago, when a little girl had walked away from her friends, from her own brother and the children who had beaten him, and bravely insisted on being his friend.

'Six weeks.' He nodded tersely and dug deep to retrieve his business self. 'I'm not running a drop-in centre, and whatever you think of my current PA it's a damn hard job. I don't do hand-holding.'

'Just put it to her. She might say no.' Costa stood while Galen still sat. 'But if she does take the job you might want to book her in with Leo and sort out her wardrobe.'

'Why?'

'Trust me on that.'

Galen could not give a damn what Roula wore. Well, so long as there were no patterns... They irritated his brain. Just that.

But she'd been in neutral colours yesterday,

apart from the blaze of red hair, and he was hardly going to ask her to dye that.

Maybe she'd ditch the name badge.

First, though, he had to speak with her.

'You're wanted,' Stephanie told Roula loudly, the second she arrived. 'There's an issue in The Temple Suite.'

'He's probably having Internet withdrawals.' Roula rolled her eyes. 'Don't worry, I'm headed there now.'

'Pretty flowers!'

'Yes.' Roula hadn't slept either. She had been into the hills and picked a gorgeous spray from the bougainvillea that draped his *yaya*'s home and had wrapped the end in wet cotton wool and some plastic. 'They're from his *yaya*'s,' Roula said. 'Hopefully it will appease him…'

Roula did not feel appeased in the least when the door to the Temple Suite opened to the sight of Galen wearing a bemused frown and not much else. She tried to ignore the fact that he was dripping wet and there was only a towel around his loins—after all, she'd seen many guests wearing less.

'Good morning!' She gave a cheery smile. 'I have moved things around so you can have the office if you choose…' He was the boss's most important guest after all. 'And I have brought the satellite phone…'

'That was quick!' Galen commented. He had clearly just got out of the shower and made the call before getting dressed. 'What are these…?' He looked at the flowers she held.

'For your *yaya*.' Roula said. 'From her home.'

'I don't think so…'

'She'll love them,' Roula insisted, holding them out at arm's length and trying not to look at him. 'It would be really nice for her.'

Reluctantly he took them. 'Please, come in.'

'As I said, I have arranged for the office—'

'Roula,' Galen cut in. 'I want to talk with you without others around. Actually…'

He stopped. She thought he must have seen her scalding cheeks.

'If you can excuse me a moment? I'll go and get dressed and maybe then we can speak.'

She turned and stood in the bright morning sun, as if it might bleach the image of his bronzed wet skin from her eyes, and the memory of the dark hairs on his chest and the glimpse of flat stomach…

She'd walked in on guests wearing practically nothing. Actually nothing at times!

Roula had seen a *lot*, working here!

But, while it might bewilder her a little, unsettle her at times, reassure her at others, this felt different.

For there had been beads of water on Galen's shoulders and arms, and as he'd taken the flowers she'd seen the darkness of his underarm hair, and she'd tried not to look at his chest, and even that had caused a certain sense of disquiet in the most unfamiliar of ways.

'Sorry about that.'

She turned at his voice.

'I honestly wasn't expecting you to get here so soon.'

He was dressed in dark linen trousers and a thin top that was a little damp, for perhaps he hadn't dried all those beads of water before pulling it on...

She fixed her smile as she spoke. 'Well, apart from the happy couple, you are currently our top guest. And you're upset...'

'No. That was just to get you here,' Galen said. 'Please, come in. Tell them my complaint was a major one! Maybe say that the flowers did the trick,' he suggested as she came in. 'Please, take a seat.'

'Thank you.' She perched on the edge of an extravagant chair. 'How has your stay been...?' Roula started, but Galen shook his head.

'Roula, my PA is soon taking six weeks' maternity leave.'

'Only six weeks?'

'I noticed how well you dealt with the wedding yesterday, especially given the short notice. I need someone like that.' Galen shrugged. 'I just thought I'd run it by you.'

'You're offering me the role of your PA?' Roula frowned.

'Yes—well, it's a short-term position, and I have to warn it's a very demanding role.'

'I don't mind demanding, but...' She swallowed. 'I'm very happy here, Galen...' Her voice trailed off as she thought of the weeks ahead and wondered if that happiness would still apply. 'My home...'

'I have a furnished apartment,' Galen said. 'I keep it for temporary staff.'

'Oh?'

'Your computer skills...?'

'Are good.' She'd been on a refresher course last month. 'Well, my passwords clearly don't suffice...' She stopped the mild joke because his expression was very serious.

'Our cyber security is way beyond what is to be expected here, but you'd be versed in that only after contracts are signed.'

'I see.'

He addressed another issue. 'Roula,' Galen said, 'if we reminisced a little too much last night...'

Her eyes flew to his. 'Did we?'

'I don't think so, but...'

Ah, the eye-meeting.

'I want to make it clear that was me on a rare day off and visiting home.'

'Of course.'

'What I am saying is that I am completely different at work. For one thing, I don't engage in small talk.'

'Small talk?'

He hesitated. 'This...'

Roula's eyes widened and she was about to say that *'this'* was just conversation. Still, their fig jam days had been long ago—he was a very different person from the one she had known then.

'Should you take this role you will have some access to my private life—mainly my grandmother and liaising with the nursing home. We are doing our best to keep her peaceful...'

'Peaceful?' Roula smiled at the irony. 'That's not the Kupia Florakis I remember—she was always very vocal.'

'Roula.' Galen spoke rather sharply. 'Perhaps I should make things a little clearer.' He looked right at her. 'An old friend might suggest I take her flowers from her home—my PA most certainly would not.'

'I see.'

'Do you?' Galen checked. 'Because for this to work that needs to be understood.'

'Galen, if you don't think I'm suitable, then why are you even offering it to me?'

'I do think you're suitable.'

Galen knew that it was then that he outright lied, for never in a million years would he hire a woman whose scent reached him from across the room, as it was doing so now, who tripped wires and crossed firm boundaries with every throaty word those full lips delivered.

Damn you, Costa!

'I am just stating how it is, and then it is for you to decide.'

Say no, he pleaded silently. Because the mystery of her dark brown eyes was too distracting for his workspace.

Say no, he pleaded silently. *Because right now I want to take you to that bed and lay you down and taste you.*

'I'm flattered...' Roula said. 'But I have commitments here. And also...'

He watched as those lips parted and she drew a breath to continue, but then those gorgeous lips closed. Worryingly for Galen, he found he *wanted* to be privy to her thoughts.

She gave him a very efficient smile. 'You understand that I need time to consider this?'

'Of course.' He moved to hand her a business card, but then seemed to change his mind and took up a pen. 'Usually all calls go through my PA,' he said, 'but this is my personal number.'

'I see.'

'If you…'

How did he say that if she needed a friend, if she was ever in Athens, or here on Anapliró, and it was all too much then she should call him? How did he resume their friendship when she might soon be working for him?

More pertinently, how did they both ignore this attraction?

And it was mutual. Galen could feel it, breathe it, almost touch it.

Yet he could not *see* it.

Her skin was pale, her eyes cool when they met his, and there was no visible sign of the vibe that thrummed in the air between them…

Galen was aware that he was not brilliant at reading people. Yet, he'd known Roula once…

Not now.

How he hated this ruse already.

'Whatever happens, you have my number.' Galen concluded the conversation and hoped that if she needed to some day then she might read between the lines.

* * *

There was little time to think about it as most of the prominent guests were helicoptered off the island and the retreat was being prepared for the next.

Late that evening—way past her rostered time—Roula checked that all was in order for the upcoming bookings. But she scrolled down and saw that, indeed, Galen's PA was due to come to Anapliró for her babymoon in two weeks' time.

And then she looked up Galen on the Internet. Gosh, she known about the platform game, but she'd had no idea how prominent he was in the tech world.

And what the hell was DeFi and Blockchain?

Working for Galen Pallas, even temporarily, really was a career opportunity. And of course the upcoming drama with Nemo made it doubly tempting…

But there was another issue to consider. One that Roula had never dealt with in any way shape or form before, because it was startling to acknowledge that she was attracted to him.

Roula hadn't just shut down that side of herself—it had never even existed. Possibly there had been a shy curiosity about her body once, but it had died on her wedding night.

And then she laughed out loud.

Gosh, she'd barely coped with a dance! Roula

knew she would run a mile from a kiss... A relationship with a man was an impossible dream at best, and from all she had learned—had been told by him, in fact—Galen was not interested in that.

And Roula was not interested in sex.

So she had a slight crush on him? Her very first.

Then again, she had seen Galen at his impressive, sociable best, groomed for a wedding.

He had told her himself he was different at work.

More, Galen made her feel...not nervous, not scared...but, just as he always had, he made her feel brave.

Roula took from her bag her rarely used phone and dialled the number he had given. Her heart was pounding when she got an automated response.

'Galen...' Roula took a breath. 'I don't think I thanked you properly for the opportunity.' She hesitated. Then, 'Yes,' she said. 'I would like to accept...'

Her time had run out, for the phone clicked off. She'd done it.

Roula stepped out into Reception a little stunned at her own boldness. Surely she should have discussed things first with Yolanda? Or her mother? Or...?

Her eyes were drawn to the occasional table and a beautiful arrangement of bougainvillea there. A frequent sight, perhaps, but she would know those blooms anywhere, for Roula had cut them herself.

'Where are these from?' she asked the cleaner, who was vacuuming.

'One of the guests left them.' She turned off the vacuum cleaner. 'I hope that's okay? It just seemed a shame to waste them.'

'Of course,' Roula agreed. 'Did the guest forget them?' she asked, while knowing it was a point-less question, for the butler would have done a sweep of the rooms. Not so much as a phone lead would be left behind by a Temple Suite guest.

'No, they were in the trash,' the cleaner said, and went back to vacuuming.

Oh, Galen...

CHAPTER SIX

FOR ALL HE KNEW, the two weeks building up to her leaving were passing slowly and for Roula. But for Galen life was on fast forward, and there was a lot to get through.

A lot!

Galen took the elevator up to his suite of offices, but frowned when he saw Kristina there, immersed in work. 'Shouldn't you be at the airport to meet Roula?'

Kristina barely looked up as she responded to his query. 'I've organised a driver.'

'Good,' Galen said, glad that it was all taken care of. Except... 'Cancel him and call my driver. I'll greet her myself.'

He was in his office when Kristina came in, and she looked startled when she saw him swigging from a bottle.

'Antacid,' Galen said, licking his chalky lips.

'Again? Do you want me to schedule an appointment...?' Kristina stopped when he shot her a look, and got to the reason why she had followed him in. 'Galen? If you want me to collect the new temp personally just say. I'm pregnant, not ill.'

'I know.' He nodded. 'But I've told the team

I'm taking today off. I'll be too busy on Monday to take Roula over to the care home...'

'I can take her over this afternoon.'

'It's no problem.'

'You're sure?' Kristina checked. 'Please don't go soft on me now, Galen.'

'I'm not.'

Galen wasn't altering his stance for Kristina, and nor would she want him to. She had insisted on working right up to the end, and no doubt had gone for her usual dawn run on the hilly Athens streets...

It wouldn't enter Kristina's head that this was...

What?

Something in Anapliró's unwritten code that you would be met at the airport? A certain rule that you greeted an old friend personally when she arrived?

Galen had long stopped following the lines in that rule book.

'Do want me to schedule Hector for next week?' Kristina asked.

'No. Tell him the wedding has derailed things...' Galen paused. 'Actually, maybe suggest dinner tonight.'

'But he's in Rome for the convention.'

'I know he is.' Galen smiled. 'At least he can't say I didn't try!'

* * *

Arrivals was busy. So busy that as his eyes skimmed the latest batch of passengers dragging their luggage Galen failed to spot Roula.

'Galen!'

He almost looked through her. In the space of two weeks, in his mind he had turned Roula into the goddess Aphrodite, with lush curves and tumbling red curls. So Galen blinked as a woman in a maroon and royal blue zig-zag skirt and a white top dotted with little circles walked towards him. Her hair was tightly scraped into a high knot and the fringe pinned tightly, as if in an attempt to squeeze every drop of colour out of it.

Galen realised then the reasoning behind Costa's warning about her clothes. For out of her smart official uniform Roula dressed... Well, even the residents in Yaya's nursing home were more up to date!

'Galen,' she said again, and gave a little wave.

Her shoes were brown, sturdy and laced, and as for her mismatched bright fabric luggage and the orange cool bag she carried... It was a drama on his eyes.

'Roula!' He righted himself. 'Welcome.'

She gave him a tense smile. 'I wasn't expecting you to meet me.'

Clearly not, Galen was about to say, but thankfully stopped himself, for her attire was completely none of his business. 'Well, there's a lot to get through. I thought we could speak in the car and stop by the care home on the way.'

As they made their way towards the waiting vehicle those zig-zags on her skirt were dancing before his eyes like a pre-migraine aura. He was irritated too by those little circles on her top, for the seams did not align. Galen could not abide patterns—even the hint of a check on a suit would have him wanting to strip it off. And of course Leo took care of all that, ensuring all his attire was plain...

'Kristina will take you to the apartment and brief you a little later.'

'She must be exhausted,' Roula said, 'working so long into her pregnancy. I have never heard of someone taking just six weeks off to have a baby—'

'Roula,' he cut in. 'I don't think it is appropriate to discuss Kristina's decision-making regarding her maternal leave.'

Plus, it made him sound like the worst boss in the world.

She felt awkward, seated in the car beside him—so awkward that she did not even take in the view.

For two weeks she had told herself that the little spark that he'd ignited would fade.

It had not.

And then she had hoped it would puff itself out on meeting him again, for surely if he was not dressed in wedding day best…?

Oh, no, it hadn't.

He wore a dark suit and a white shirt and a gunmetal tie, and his jaw was unshaven. And he was even more beautiful than she had remembered, or dared now acknowledge.

'How was your trip?' he enquired politely, in a voice rich and deep with the vibration of a purr.

'Long.'

'Long?' Galen checked. He had thought, given the circumstances, that Costa would have arranged a comfortable passage. 'Didn't you take the chopper to Thira?'

'The helicopter is for guests, Galen.'

'Of course.' He took a breath. Now that he thought about it, Costa would not be wanting to raise any flags with the locals. 'Look, if you want to go to the apartment first, freshen up, have a break…'

Change out of that skirt!

'No.' She shook her head. 'We agreed I'd start at two. I came ready to hit the ground running.'

Or to go hiking! Very deliberately, he did not look at her shoes.

* * *

'How was it?' Galen asked her. 'Your leaving?'

'It was…' Roula even opened her mouth to tell him about her hellish two weeks, yet quickly pulled back. 'Fine.'

However, it seemed Galen really wanted to hear how she was. 'Roula, you're not working for me yet.'

'No, and before we commence work I thought I could give you this.' She pointed to the little cool bag she'd been carrying. 'It's just some cheese from home, *chlorotiri*, and some *melitzanosalata* that I made last night—for your grandmother…'

'You didn't have to do that.'

'I would *always* do that.' Roula smiled. 'You can take the girl out of Anapliró, but you can never…' Then she felt a little embarrassed by his discomfort over her small gift. 'If that is over-stepping the mark…?'

'It's not that. We're trying to keep her calm…' Galen explained. 'Peaceful. Any talk of Anapliró only confuses her.'

'So you don't mention it?'

He looked at her then, their first real eye contact since meeting, and she saw there was a warning in his eyes. 'I do all I can to avoid upsetting her,' he clipped.

'Of course.'

'I should also warn you that she gets confused

at times. It varies. She can be very lucid, but there are times she thinks I'm my father. At other times I am ten, or...' He ran a finger around his shirt collar. 'She can be a little personal.'

'It's fine.'

'I apologise in advance.'

They drove on in silence. Roula twisted a strand of hair that had escaped rather than bite her nails. They passed the very police station where she had given the statement that would condemn her brother.

'We're here,' Galen said.

There were no care homes on Anapliró, but even so, this was not how Roula had envisaged one. Really, it was more like stepping into a five-star hotel from a glossy magazine. There were glamorous elders chatting in a lounge to one side, as if taking high tea, and there was even someone playing the piano.

'Galen!' A very sprightly man held up his stick.

'Sir!' Galen nodded.

The staff were all immaculate, though they appeared a little surprised to see him.

'Galen! We weren't expecting you today.'

'This is Roula,' Galen introduced her. 'From Monday you will be liaising with her.'

'Of course. It's nice to meet you.'

'Likewise.' Roula smiled, and listened as they brought Galen up to date.

'Kupia Florakis is still refusing to dress and is really quite distressed. We are about to give her something a little stronger than her usual medication. Would you like me to take you through?'

'I know the way.'

He was coming across as abrupt—but then, Roula recalled, that was Galen. He dealt in facts and of course he didn't need an escort.

'How often do you manage to visit?' she asked, assuming from the staff's evident surprise that his appearances here were rare.

She had assumed wrong, Roula quickly realised.

'I try to take coffee with her most days during the week, though I don't generally come on a Friday. I prefer to work uninterrupted over the weekend.'

Roula was shocked when she saw Kupia Florakis dressed in her nightwear and standing rubbing the window, as if to clear it, as two staff tried to tempt her to a chair.

Gosh, she was so tiny. Or was it that Galen was so tall as he walked over to her?

'Hey…' he said, joining her at the window.

'It's gone!' Even her voice had shrunk.

'It hasn't gone,' Galen said.

'It's all disappeared into the sea…'

'No, no…' Galen gently refuted. 'I work over

there.' He pointed. 'And you are here so that I can see you more.'

Her room was beautiful, and there were multiple photos on the shelves, but Roula's eyes were drawn to one of Galen in his military uniform. Her gaze darted away, back to where Galen was now guiding his *yaya*.

'Come and sit. I have someone for you to meet.'

She ran a hand over the arm his dark suit. 'Are you here for a funeral?'

'No funeral,' Galen said.

'Your tie should be black,' she said as he led her to a seat.

'Yaya, this is Roula,' he introduced her. 'You might see her a bit over the next few weeks.'

'Kupia Florakis,' Roula smiled. 'It is nice to...' She hesitated, for surely she should say that it was nice to see her again, rather than deny knowing her. 'It's good to see you.'

Galen watched as his *yaya* turned her currant eyes to Roula, and then he watched as she did what he must not. She reached up and took hold of the single strand of hair that she had been twirling.

'Kyrios?' Yaya said.

'Yes.' Roula nodded, but did not glance over to see Galen's reaction to the fact that she had been recognised, albeit by her previous name.

Yaya looked her slowly up and down and then turned to Galen. 'Roula shopped for me.'

'Did she?' Galen took a breath. 'I didn't know that.'

'Well, you were gone,' Kupia Florakis rebuked him. 'No help. Go back to your books Galen.' Now she looked back to Roula and tapped the side of her head. 'He's not right up here. The doctor said. Damaged.'

Roula saw the tension behind his smile as he ignored her cruel words, and, yes, she might be confused now, but Roula rather guessed Galen might have heard much the same growing up.

'Roula brought you this,' Galen said, and opened the glowing cool bag. 'Come on,' he said gently. 'Eat.'

But Kupia Florakis hadn't finished with her observations yet, and she looked over to Roula.

'What happened to you? You were so pretty once.'

Galen tried to distract her with the cheese.

'Why is she hiding?'

'Yaya…' Galen said as Roula stood, her face one burning blush.

'She's so ugly now.'

The nurse came in then. It was pill time for his *yaya*, it would seem.

To her shame, Roula felt somewhat relieved, for she felt more than a little exposed.

'She says things...' Galen said, and he sighed once they were back in the car, leaning back on the headrest, his eyes closed for a moment. 'You know, she spent the first decade of my life telling me to engage my filter before I spoke, and the last decade has been spent...' He opened his eyes and looked over at her then. 'I'm sorry if she was rude. I have to buy flowers for the staff all the time to apologise.'

'No flowers required.' She smiled back.

'She doesn't mean half of it...'

'I know that.' Roula nodded.

But it was the half that was true which burnt...

Kolonaki Square was beautiful.

'Leo's studio is over there,' Galen said. 'You're more than welcome to get a new work wardrobe...'

'I have plenty of clothes, Galen.'

Her response was a little acidic, but with every sentence spoken the division between them grew wider. He flew—she took the ferry. He dressed in designer clothes and turned heads—she...

Oh, it was more than that, though, and the division actually helped. Even walking through the square, she was aware of him in such an unfamiliar way.

'Unless you *prefer* your staff to be dressed by Leo Arati?'

'Kristina asked for it to be in her contract. I was just...' He shrugged and nodded to a doorman, who opened one of the old wooden doors.

And there the square evaporated.

The ancient building was still there, but its imperfections had somehow been enhanced. Stone walls were exposed, and old windows too, yet there were glass cloisters and elevators, and it was so vast it felt as if she was looking up to a spaceship.

'It's stunning,' Roula croaked.

It was so much more than that.

'It's a bit confusing at first,' Galen warned as they walked past a security guard. 'Costa's got the second floor, though he's still on honeymoon. And my development team's main workspace is through there...'

She looked at the handful of people behind glass, all working away and completely oblivious to them.

'There are also private offices on my floor. I'm sure Kristina will explain.'

He showed her the codes to the glass elevators and that felt overwhelming, but then she recalled her terror on her first day of work at the retreat.

She could do this.

'Roula, this is Kristina.'

'Welcome!'

Kristina was indeed dressed by Leo Arati!

For her last day in the office she wore a little black dress, and her make-up was so 'after-five' she would have parted a velvet rope anywhere. Even her baby bump, though large for her petite frame, seemed to want to oblige, and was so neat and round that it fully deserved its own little bow—not that she would ever wear one.

I want to be her, Roula thought. Well, not specifically Kristina, but she wanted to wear red lipstick as if she simply always did, and to own every part of herself as she crossed a room.

For a moment Kristina discussed a dinner booking with Galen, and then she addressed Roula. 'This will be your office—well, after today...' Kristina smiled a very brittle smile.

'Oh,' Roula said, as she looked at the bare surroundings. There was so much glass she felt as if she stood inside an ice cube. 'You didn't have to clear out your personal effects and things...'

'I didn't,' Kristina said tartly. 'I like a tidy space. I'll give you a tour and a rundown, then take you to the apartment.' She glanced to Galen. 'We'll be fine.'

'Well, very best wishes,' Galen said. 'I hope all goes well.'

'Thank you.' Roula smiled.

'I think he was talking to me,' Kristina said rather pointedly. 'Thanks, Galen. I guess I'll see you in six weeks.'

That was it? Roula tried not to gape at this very matter-of-fact farewell. Gosh, at the retreat if a member of staff was leaving to have a baby—well, it was a wonder that any work got done on that day!

And this was his personal assistant!

Kristina made no attempt at conversation as she packed up her bag.

'So are you all out celebrating tonight...?' Roula attempted brightly, wondering if that was the dinner booking that she had mentioned.

'Sorry?' Kristina glanced up.

'The dinner?'

'Roula, may I be blunt?'

'Go ahead.'

'You worked for Costa, yes?'

'Correct—well, Yolanda was my direct boss...'

'I know he has several hotels, but it's a family business—yes?'

Roula nodded.

'Well, this *isn't* a family business,' Kristina warned her. 'If I want a cake and a party, then I'll ask my husband or my friends.'

Roula considered herself told!

The whole place—including the people—were

just so cold. It was beautiful, but so clinical Roula was sure a forensics team would struggle to find a fingerprint, let alone signs of life.

'This is the guest lounge,' Kristina said. 'But there is another downstairs. I prefer visitors to wait down there.'

All the staff were so engrossed they barely looked up as she was shown around. There was an open-plan staff lounge, but no one was gathered there. Perhaps because their boss's office was opposite, and most of the doors were glass.

Not that Galen looked up.

He was a man of many screens! Roula counted six as they passed.

'Nico…' Kristina introduced her to a young man. 'This is Roula.'

He barely looked up, just mumbled, 'Hi…'

'Now I'll take you to Dora, the laziest woman on God's earth. She'll be playing games online, but the second she sees us…'

Sure enough, Dora reminded Roula of her nieces when they were pretending to do their homework. Except Dora was in her fifties and her curls were grey. She jolted to attention and pretended to be busy as she quickly closed down her screen in the same way the twins did.

'Dora,' Kristina said, in a very bored voice. 'This is Roula, my temporary replacement. I've told her that if she has any problems she is to come to you.'

'Of course.' Dora smiled. 'It's lovely to meet you, Roula.'

'Thank you,' Roula said as she received her first real smile since her arrival. 'Likewise.'

'Dora?' Kristina soon broke the pleasant exchange. 'Can you please get off whatever game you're wasting time on and sort out Nico's leave, and then chase HR for Roula's contract…?'

'I was actually just doing that.'

Kristina gave a scoffing laugh, but stopped as her phone bleeped. 'Galen wants me.'

'He *texts* you?' Roula checked—because they were literally a few steps away from his office, should he deign to look up.

'Of course,' Kristina said.

Roula's jaw gaped as Kristina, as if she was training a puppy, told her to 'Stay!'

No, she did not want to be Kristina any more.

'She's like that with everyone.'

Roula turned as Dora unwrapped a chocolate ball.

'Don't take it personally…'

Who were these people who texted and offended, but took no offence…?

Oh, she wanted to be back in Anapliró, where at least at work she knew who she was and was the best at her job…

* * *

In fairness, most of the time Galen had no idea where Kristina was in the building, and texting her was an efficient method of communication.

The trouble today was that he knew exactly where Kristina was—or rather Roula.

'Galen?' Kristian checked.

'Perhaps take Roula over to the apartment now?'

'I'm just showing her around while I wait for HR to send over her contract.'

'Maybe take her now.'

'Sure.' Kristina turned to go, but then turned back. 'Galen, I just want to say... Well, both Ruben and I want to...'

'Can we please drop it?' Galen said, for he had made it clear more than a year ago, when he'd paid for his loyal PA and her husband to be treated by Athens's top IVF specialist, that he would prefer the fact not to be raised. 'I'm thrilled you finally got there. Well, aside from the fact that I am now destined to six weeks of zig-zags.'

Kristina laughed. 'Do you want me to tell Roula about your issue with patterns?'

'Are we even allowed to do that now?' He rolled his eyes. 'Or will we offend the pattern police?'

'We need you to be working, Galen. I'll have a word.'

'Good. Now get the hell out of here and go and have your baby.'

Roula watched as Kristina gave Galen a half-wave and then marched her efficient way over.

'We should get over to the apartment.'

'Kristina…' Roula was starting to have serious doubts, both about her suitability and her qualifications, and decided it might be better to just state it now. 'I don't think I'm cut out—'

'Let's discuss this at the apartment.'

The apartment was in a very narrow lane, so the driver dropped them a short walk away and they made their way down.

'It's a nice location,' Kristina said as she clipped along.

Nice?

It was on the edge of everything.

The beautiful church of Aghios Dionysios was close. There were cafés, restaurants, boutiques… a whole new world at her door…

'This is yours.'

They climbed a steep staircase with detailed iron rails—a gorgeous slice of old Athens.

'Ground floor,' Kristina said as she let them in and they walked down a long, high-ceilinged corridor. 'This one's yours. Just the one bedroom…'

Kristina snapped on the lights and opened all the doors, speaking like a realtor. 'It's serviced weekly...'

It was beautiful. The apartment alone almost tempted her to stay and fake it until she made it—or whatever the saying was.

Roula looked out of the bedroom window.

'No views,' Kristina said.

Oh, but there were. There were people and cafés and life pulsing outside. Except...

'I'm really not sure I'm qualified.'

'You're overwhelmed?'

'Yes,' she admitted. 'I told Galen I was computer literate, and until now I honestly thought I was, but...'

'Roula, when I was interviewed for this role I insisted that I wanted the title of Executive Assistant. But, as Galen pointed out, it would be a lie. I have degrees in both business and computer science, and yet I still don't really understand what the hell he does.'

'Oh...'

'He's a genius,' Kristina said. 'And I don't say that lightly. There are a few of them working there.'

Roula nodded, and there was a quiet sadness as the truth was acknowledged. Galen had been called so many things growing up. Different...

odd…damaged… And today she had found out that his *yaya* had clearly thought he was too.

'I run the edges of Galen's life so that he can do more of what he's good at. That role will be yours, while I…' Kristina gestured to her stomach. 'So, shall we go through everything and then you can decide if you're up to it or not?'

Roula found that she rather admired Kristina's directness and, despite appearances to the contrary, there truly was kindness in her, for she had waited until they were well away from the office to address this.

'Yes,' Roula said, ready to hear more about the role.

'Okay…' They both took a seat and Roula got out a new notebook and pen. 'Galen has to do corporate stuff for the gaming Tuesday to Thursday—he hates it. That's when you'll appear to be busy.'

'Appear…?'

'Lots of phone calls, sitting in meetings—just all the usual. There's a big ball coming up…' She waved that fact away. 'But I should be back on board by then. And there's a new release. The directors are pushing Galen for progress reports, so they can announce it. What you need to understand is that everything corporate and/or family falls in that Tuesday to Thursday timeline. Today is an anomaly. Usually on Friday he has a development team meeting at seven a.m....'

'Do I need to be there for that?'

'I'm always there at six. The café delivers breakfast, but you don't need to stay for the meeting, thank goodness—they eat like horses at the trough.' Kristina pulled a face. 'Usually they all go off, and then Galen locks himself in his office and does all his programming and coding.' She held up her hands. 'Don't disturb him for *any* reason.'

'Got it.'

'I mean it. You don't have to be in the office, but Galen's phone lines will be diverted to you, so that *nothing* interrupts him—well, apart from one.' She fixed Roula with a look. 'Unless his *yaya* is actually dead, or very soon to be, just deal with it. The care home will call all the time.' Kristina rolled her eyes and moved swiftly along. 'On Mondays Galen is awful—just bring in coffee, put it down, leave. At some point he'll rise from the ashes... What else...?' Kristina thought out loud. 'Sex and food.'

Roula let her pen hover over the paper.

'He gets food and coffee delivered all the time—I mean *all the time*. Just take it from the driver, put it on his desk. He won't look up.'

'Okay...' Roula looked at her list. *Grow up,*

Roula. You deal with stuff like this at the retreat.
She'd had to find a vibrator for a client once!
'What about…?'

'Sex? Oh, don't worry, he factors that in himself. Thankfully I don't have to run that.'

'So I just order flowers and book restaurants and such?'

'God, no.' Kristina shook her head. 'His lovers are as practical about it as he is. That's the one phone line he keeps open, but if you get a text from one of them by mistake, just text back "PA".'

'How will I know it's one of them?'

'They'll say "Bored?" or "Catch-up?" That sort of thing. Don't worry, there's nothing lewd.' Kristina shrugged. 'Honestly, it's not an issue. Also, if he disappears for a couple of days, that's probably why.'

Gosh.

'Or if there's an afternoon when you can't find him.'

'I see.'

'Or…'

'I get it, thank you.'

There was also his doorman, whom she could call if any dire events occurred while Galen was missing!

Roula's usually neat lists were pages of scribble by the time Kristina was through.

'Look, if you have any doubts,' Kristina said

as she stood, 'particularly when he's in lockdown programming, run them by me—don't disturb him.'

'You're sure? But you're…' Roula honestly wasn't sure if she was allowed to mention that Kristina was clearly very close to being due!

'Absolutely.'

'Thanks for being so thorough.'

'Well, it's best to know what you're getting into. Your time will no longer be yours, but if you don't want the position say so now—believe me, there are many who do. I have three people I usually fall back on…'

Roula knew she was being warned that this really was a coveted job.

'I just had a wobble back at the office,' Roula admitted.

'I get it,' Kristina said. 'But you wobble in here—not there.'

'Noted.'

'I'll leave you to settle in,' she said, but as she clipped towards the door she turned around. 'Bring his coffee from the café on Monday, remember?'

'Got it,' Roula said, and read back his complicated order. She frowned when Kristina pressed her thumb and fingers to her forehead. 'Are you…?' Gosh, was she even allowed to ask? 'Is everything…?'

'I have a headache. I've had it since last night…'

Kristina suddenly didn't look quite so photo-shoot-ready—she looked as if she might faint.

'Kristina, sit down,' Roula told her.

'Don't say anything to Galen.'

'I shan't.'

Roula didn't quite know what to do with this very private, very bristly woman, but she quickly worked out the complicated curtains and they sat in semi darkness.

Kristina took off her heels and lay on the couch. 'Excuse me,' she said, and then admitted, 'I'm embarrassed. I don't tend to lie down at work. Ruben would freak if I told him that I'm having headaches. My husband,' she added.

'Would you like me to leave you?'

'It's fine…' Kristina said. 'I'll go in a moment… the driver's waiting…' She grimaced as her phone buzzed.

'Let me…' Roula offered, and took the phone. But she blinked as she read the message.

'The care home?' Kristina checked, without opening her eyes.

'No, it's Galen, asking if you've told me about my "awful zig-zag skirt".'

Kristina gave a soft laugh. 'He hates patterns. They cause some kind of overload to his brain. Don't be offended.'

'I'm not.' In fact, it cleared things up a little as

she thought back to the bed linen and her opinion that he was picky and precious. That he'd changed.

Maybe he hadn't completely changed, Roula realised. Perhaps she just knew him a little more.

And Roula also knew what her guest services manager self would do...

'Kristina, why don't I tell the driver we'll be a while and that you'll call him when you're ready to be picked up?'

'You don't mind?'

'Of course not.'

Kristina dozed for a full hour, and Roula sat, a little awkward in her new home, looking at the late afternoon sky and the pile of suitcases waiting to be unpacked.

Most of them were full of things she had retrieved from his *yaya*'s home—though it would seem that wasn't allowed in this cold, get-ahead world.

Roula's own phone chimed loudly and, expecting it to be her mother, she swallowed when she saw that it was Galen.

How's Kristina?

She looked over to Kristina, who had stirred and come awake at the sound of Roula's unfamiliar and loud phone.

'It's Galen,' Roula said. 'Asking how we're getting on.'

'Shh…' Kristina put a finger to her lips.

Roula texted back.

Wonderful.

'Thanks for that.' Kristina sat up and drank the water Roula had placed next to her. 'I feel a lot better. I'll call the driver and head back.' She nodded when she saw Roula's worried face. 'I'll call my doctor.'

'Good.'

It was odd but they seemed to be…well, not friends, exactly, but a lot friendlier as Kristina left.

And it was odder still to stand alone in the apartment that was now her temporary home. It was gorgeous, with a beautiful bathroom and a gleaming kitchen, but it was the bedroom she paused in. The bed was high, and dressed in smart white cotton with a shot of silk through it, and the pillows were plump.

It had been a very long time since Roula had slept in a bed. And a whole lot longer than that since she'd enjoyed sleeping in one!

She opened a window and took in the sounds of the city on a Friday evening. Traffic and people—all there on her doorstep. Roula was a little too nervous to venture out, but then her phone buzzed again, and she saw it was Galen.

'Galen?'

'Sorry about this… I have dinner with a client tonight. It's unexpected, but…'

'It's fine.' Roula smiled at his attempt to be polite. 'I didn't expect you to entertain me on my first night.'

'This isn't a social call. Kristina isn't available, so you'll have to come with me.'

She winced at her own presumption. 'What time?'

'Now,' Galen said. 'Well, by the time you get up the lane the car will be there. Also,' Galen added, 'we need to speak.'

CHAPTER SEVEN

'I DID WARN YOU the job was full-on,' Galen said as she climbed into the car.

'You did.'

'And I'm aware that you haven't signed your contract yet.' He held up a folder. 'We can go through that after dinner—hopefully it won't drag on. The guest is Hector,' he explained. 'Chairman of the board. I didn't think he'd actually fly in.'

He pressed the intercom and spoke to his driver, and Roula went a little pale as the driver confirmed that they were on schedule.

'Galen?' She was taken aback when she heard the name of the restaurant they were headed to. It was such an exclusive restaurant that even for the retreat guests reservations were not always able to be secured! 'You should have said where we were going?'

'Why? It's just dinner.'

For him, perhaps.

No wonder Kristina was photoshoot-ready, Roula thought as they drove up the hill. Then again, the only halfway decent dress she had was black—the one she used for funerals. Another hand-me-down from her mother.

Roula sighed, but then snapped to attention as Galen spoke on.

'Hector wants to find out if there's any progress on Game Four.'

'The Anapliró game?'

'It's not Anapliró,' Galen corrected. 'Just loosely based on it. Anyway, he's really pushy.' He told her what Kristina already had. 'They want to announce the release date at the ball.'

'Is it nowhere near ready?'

'I'm not discussing that until your contract's signed.'

That stung a little too much, but Roula took a breath and reminded herself of the warning Galen himself had delivered—he was very different at work. They were not friends going out or catching up.

Roula was so underdressed for such fine dining that she actually did turn heads. A nudge when they saw Galen…a gape for Roula. Her face was actually burning as they were ushered to a table—or rather, one of *the* tables…

As the waiter held out her chair Roula attempted a little joke to Galen as she took her seat. 'Best tuck my skirt away!'

'Sorry?' Galen frowned.

'I saw your message to Kristina about it.'

'Oh!' He grimaced. 'I asked Kristina to broach my issue with patterns.'

'You could have just said.'

'Well, I find those sorts of topics difficult,'

Galen admitted. 'I'm not allowed to notice Kristina's girth or she gets annoyed.'

Roula gave a little laugh.

'Don't order a starter,' he warned. 'I don't want this to drag on.'

'Okay.' She looked over. 'What about dessert?'

'Hopefully he won't last that long,'

The glug of wine being poured welcomed Roula on this, her first night in Athens. Yet they sat pretty much in silence as she turned and drank in the view, for it was as if they were seated on the edge of heaven, encased by hills with the sea beyond, the centrepiece the beautiful citadel and its gorgeous ancient buildings.

'Gosh!' Roula sighed. 'It beats the school trip.'

Galen didn't respond. He was checking his phone. 'Someone is ill on Hector's plane and they can't disembark,' he said.

'You seem pleased?'

'I am—it's usually me cancelling him.' He looked over to the approaching waiter. 'Could you give us a moment, please?'

'Are we leaving?' Roula checked, assuming the night was over.

'No, no,' Galen said. 'I told you that we need to speak… Did Kristina explain everything?'

'Yes.' Roula nodded. 'She was very thorough.'

'Any concerns?' he asked. 'Because now is the time to air them.'

'I don't think so.' Roula shook her head. While there was no way she would be able to work for him permanently, she was only here for six weeks. She could survive in the fridge where he worked for that long. 'As I said, she was very thorough. Though it's Friday—shouldn't you be locked in your office now?'

'I'll be headed there soon.' He nodded. 'It's been one of those days. One PA leaving…another one arriving.'

'Yes.'

'I actually have some concerns myself, Roula,' Galen said, and though his voice was calm and even there was no mistaking a certain edge to his tone. 'Kristina is, as we speak, in hospital, strapped to monitors.'

Roula's eyes flashed up as she realised she'd been caught lying on her first day. 'Is she okay?'

'Well, she's certainly not "wonderful", as you made out. I specifically asked you how she was.'

'Galen, I thought you were just messaging to see how it was all going,' Roula admitted. 'If we were getting along…'

'Why would I care if two professionals who will never see each other again are getting along?' he asked, clearly irritated. 'Do you think I suddenly looked up and thought, *Oh, I hope they are having a nice time*…' He shook his head in frustrated annoyance. 'I messaged you to ask how Kristina was. You should have told me.'

'You really want me to tell you when a staff member has a headache?' Roula checked. 'I didn't think it was that kind of place.'

'Excuse me?'

Roula was assertive at work. 'It's clear your staff leave their private lives at the door,' she said.

'Don't we all?' he said. 'Or do you smile like that at home?'

'Like what?'

He flashed her an odd bright smile and then halted. 'Look, I get why you didn't tell me,' he conceded. 'She's nearly due, though.'

'Yes.'

'My driver returned concerned, so I texted you to see how she was.'

'I see that now.'

Subject closed.

'Shall we get menus?'

'Sure.'

Not quite closed.

'Roula, I overreacted. But it was clearly panic stations for Kristina.'

'Can you find out how she is?'

'Ruben said he will call.'

'Will you let me know?'

He nodded. 'Nico would *not* make a good doula.'

Roula found that she was smiling, and not her corporate one. There were unfamiliar muscles stretching her lips as they parted over her teeth, and she could actually feel the edge of the top row on her mouth.

As they looked through the menus his gaze fell on the plaster on her middle finger. She'd worn one last week, but it had been on her thumb, and that was still there too. Galen noticed such things.

He guessed she was biting her nails.

'The calamari is amazing here...' Galen suggested.

'I hate fish.'

'Not brilliant if your husband's a fisherman...' Galen stopped. He really was awful at jokes and that had been a dreadful attempt.

'Risotto,' she said, and then added, 'Please.'

They were awkward. Impossibly so.

She had gone through her contract for the retreat with Costa, in the retreat's restaurant. And Leo always treated her to a lovely lunch whenever they caught up. What was this? Roula asked herself.

But she knew...

She'd never dined with a man she was attracted to.

Had never known this feeling at all.

'How are you, Roula?' he asked when their meals had been served. 'Really?'

She looked up. 'I thought we weren't going to engage in idle conversation.'

'You haven't signed the contract,' Galen pointed out. 'Maybe, just for tonight, we can catch up? How were your family about you leaving?'

'A little upset,' Roula admitted. 'They don't believe it's just for six weeks.'

'Is it?'

Gosh, a real conversation—it had been a long time since she'd had one of those. 'I don't know,' Roula admitted. 'For now, I'm on leave from the retreat. Yolanda was a little cross at first. She said I'd given no indication...' She shrugged. 'You know what it can be like when staff leave.'

'Not really.' He tore some bread. 'I can't get rid of mine.' He gave her a half-smile, a little sad that she clearly felt unable to tell him about her brother. 'We might seem cold at first, but you should give us a chance.'

'Yes,' Roula agreed, for this job really was a serious opportunity. 'I should.' But first... 'How are *you*, Galen?'

'I'm trying to make you feel welcome, Roula.'

'So tell me how you've been.'

'I've been well.'

'How was the military?'

'That was years ago.' He cast his mind back. 'It was good. I liked the training, and I got to fix computers instead of mopping and cleaning. After that I settled in Athens. I went back to Anapliró a couple of times to visit my *yaya*.'

'I heard.' She looked at him then, and Galen found that he was frowning at her expression, for she looked a little cross.

'She often spoke about you.'

He didn't want to visit the past. 'Right, shall we do this?' He opened the file he had brought along and pushed it across the table. He took out his pen and Roula looked at the contract.

It was just a contract.

Generous, but not some major cash dump for an old friend from Anapliró, and her accommodation was a separate contract for an eight-week term.

'A couple of weeks' leeway,' Galen explained. 'So you're not looking for both a new job and a place to live.'

'That's very thoughtful.'

'I can be.'

He smiled, and Roula did not know what to do, for she had never known a smile to have such effect.

She was acutely aware that she was probably the worst-dressed woman in the restaurant, yet when he smiled at her she felt almost a little beautiful…and a little bit teary too.

She did not know what this was.

Did not know how, when he pointed out a line on the contract, his finger seemed still to be before her eyes long after it had left the page.

Perhaps Galen was her version of seeing pattern, because this was sensory overload, and Roula did not know what to do with it all.

She even liked his gentle chiding as he tutted when she told him, 'I don't want a bonus in crypto currency.'

'Philistine!' he teased, and then added, 'Roula, it's a minor detail.'

'Well, I'd rather have cash.'

'We call it fiat currency—however, the "cash" equivalent wouldn't pay for a glass of wine at the moment,' Galen said. 'It's more a morale thing to do with the potential of the project…'

She picked up the pen and it felt cold and heavy in her hands. 'I'm having a wobble,' she admitted. 'According to Kristina, I should only have them at home.'

'Then take it home to read,' Galen said, and she watched as his hand returned. She felt the warm brush of his fingers as he took the weight of the pen, yet she felt no lighter. Instead she felt heavy with indecision, for it was no longer the job that felt challenging, but the six weeks in close proximity to Galen she was struggling with. Or rather, her new companion: awareness.

Such awareness.

And not just for the man who sat before her, but of her own body in the chair. She prickled all over, as if tiny shards of glass were working their way to the surface of her skin, not so much pain, more a rising presence.

And so, instead of signing, she nodded in relief at the waiter's suggestion they move to the balcony to enjoy their coffee.

Only there was no relief there, for they were guided to a plump couch to savour the sunset.

'Still better than the school trip?' Galen said, as pinks blazed in the sky and the temples were lit on the sacred stone, and in the distance the Aegean turned shifting purple.

'So much better.' Roula sighed. 'This is surely the best view on earth.'

'Truth?' he said. 'I prefer the view from my home. A different angle, but...'

'You're so arrogant!' She half laughed.

'Am I?'

'I don't know...' Roula admitted.

She didn't know!

She was remembering him—remembering Galen who said things as they were, and offended at times, but was always kind.

He was the most honest person she'd ever

known. At times so direct it was confrontational. And yet there was a rare sense of security to be found in that too. Truth.

'There was snow here this winter…' Galen said as she gazed out.

'I heard.' Roula nodded, though she did not turn her head—for who would turn away as the setting sun seemed to set the Parthenon on fire?

She wanted to turn her head, though. So much so her neck felt taut.

'I woke up,' Galen told her, 'and I had never heard Athens so silent.'

'Truly?'

'I walked around in it for hours.'

She could feel his breath, and his thigh was against hers, and still Roula stared ahead. Because her neck ached to turn, but her mind told her she would ruin things. That he would laugh in her face if she moved in to kiss him, for she was surely misreading things?

It wasn't even the fact that he was soon to be her boss that was the issue right now.

For even if he did not laugh in her face…even if he moved to kiss her back…she wouldn't know what to do.

This new want, this genesis of desire, was too much and too soon. She wanted to want from a distance, not seated by his side.

'I should get back,' Roula said as the sky slipped into night. 'I had a very early start today.'

'Of course.'

He got a call on the way out, and it was good news.

'Kristina is fine,' he told her. 'She has to have her blood pressure checked again, but the baby-moon is on.'

'I'm so pleased. You should call Nico.'

'I'll tell him when I get back to the office.'

The drive home was a silent one except for the drum of his fingers on the walnut trim as Galen pondered how it must feel for Roula to be in a new city, in a new workplace, and to know that any day now her life would become headline news.

And, while he chose not to get involved in the dramas of other people's lives, he felt a reluctant yet definite responsibility.

She really was on her own.

'Roula…' As they neared the apartment he turned and saw the lights of the city flash on her pale cheeks. 'We used to talk, yes?'

'Yes.'

'On Monday things change,' Galen said. 'As I said when I offered you the role, things are different at work, but that doesn't mean…' *Merda,* he was bad at this. The car pulled in at the top of the lane. 'I'll walk you down.'

'There's no need.'

'We're not on Anapliró now.'

Tell me, Roula, Galen thought as they walked down the lane in tense silence.

'Thank you for dinner,' Roula said as they came to the steps. 'And for meeting me this morning.'

She was getting out the keys, about to go in and face this alone.

'Yolanda's right,' Galen said. 'You give no indication as to what's going on with you.'

Roula swallowed. 'Perhaps its wiser not to.'

'Tell me, Roula.'

'I think it's better I don't.'

'Surely you know you can tell me anything?'

'Anything?' Roula checked.

Once she had trusted him in a way that was hard to define. Once she'd been able to share what was on her mind with him, and Galen was inviting her to do so again now.

He had been her first real friend.

Her first dance—well, the first that she'd enjoyed…

And now, for the first time in her life, she wanted a kiss. It felt like a butterfly flitting past, and it was so fleeting, so rare, so impossible, that she was scared the feeling might never come again.

Roula had taken notes on his sex life this afternoon—she knew how little one kiss would mean to him.

Yet it would mean the world to her. To know...

'I want to be kissed goodnight,' Roula admitted. '*That* is what is on my mind.'

He looked at her. Hell, he had meant her just to tell him about all the drama going on with your brother.

'You want me to kiss you?' he checked.

'Yes, but if you kiss me here, can we end it there? I mean, I won't ask you in.'

A kiss?

Two weeks ago he would have laughed at the thought of just a kiss—at least on the inside— but he guessed it would be her first since her husband.

'Sure.' He was practical. 'But then we're done.'

'Completely.'

Roula felt his hands on her arms and breathed in, in nervous preparation for his mouth. Except it was the softest brush of lips, and she felt as if there must be snow in May, for Athens had become silent.

There was nothing she could liken it to, for

it was soft and slow, and yet it made that deep breath pointless, for she was hungry for air when his kiss did not end with that brush of lips.

The pressure of his mouth was a relief, and as his hands moved from her arms to her head she felt his fingers in her thick hair. Then it was Roula who parted her lips, and the slip of his tongue was the most beautiful thing she had ever known.

It was like dancing, and it was like laughing, and it stroked her and gently coaxed her, until her hands were in his hair.

This was how it felt to be kissed, to kiss, to want the touch of another.

His fingers stroked her back and moved to her bra strap—or rather straps, because she felt them linger to check. And then his hand moved down, his arm circling her waist, and for a second she opened her eyes.

His eyes were closed, so Roula returned to the darkness, and the deep, deep kiss, and the citrussy clean scent of him, and the slow thrill of his tongue and the mouth that made her want more.

And then he ended it.

Their mouths shiny and wet, her skin a little raw, they stood, bodies apart, heads together, both breathless.

'Go in,' Galen told her, and his voice was a touch uneven.

She knew that in his world they should be up against a wall now, with her legs wrapped around him. Yet for Roula everything felt right with the world.

She stood and savoured her first kiss—well, the first kiss she had enjoyed—simply lingering in the ripe deliciousness of it.

'Thank you,' she said.

'My pleasure.' Galen nodded. 'We might do it again on your leaving day, but not a moment before.'

Roula laughed as he walked off.

Then he abruptly turned and walked right up to her, but it did not feel confrontational…it felt necessary. 'Roula.'

'Yes?'

'Wear zig-zags.'

She frowned.

'Spots, stripes…'

They were staring at each other, and it was both tense and a relief to be lost in his eyes and to see that their kiss had affected him.

'Whatever you've got in that luggage…'

'Will do.'

She took for ever though to sort out the unfamiliar keys and get inside the door, and from there she gave him a wave. 'See you on Monday.'

'Yes,' Galen said.

In stripes, spots *and* zig-zags, preferably!

CHAPTER EIGHT

ROULA'S PHONE BLEEPED. And then it gave another bleep, and it took her a moment to work out quite where she was.

In bed.

The cover was heavy, the pillow soft, and she lay on her stomach and flicked off the alarm, then lay there.

She *had* contemplated male beauty before.

Once.

That photo of Galen in uniform she had seen long ago. In fact it had been years old by the time she'd even seen it.

'Is this Galen?' she had asked, and smiled, looking at the picture as she dropped off Kupia Florakis's shopping. Studious, happy, hopeful for her exams and not really interested in boys, she'd been feeling a shy curiosity over her body she had deliberately ignored.

Or she had tried to.

Yet that photo had somehow embedded itself and hooked in her mind...

One morning, weeks, perhaps months after she'd dropped off that shopping, Roula had awoken to a loud knock on her bedroom door, hauling her back from a place she did not know. A place in her dreams of torrid, rough kisses and heated skin and no trace of her usual shyness as Galen boldly explored her.

'Roula!'

Her mother had told her she'd be late for school even as she'd lain there, breathless, aware of a heavy heat between her legs and wishing the morning had not invaded just yet, for she wanted to get back to that place she'd glimpsed.

'I'm up...' Roula had croaked, and although perhaps guilt should have propelled her from the bed she'd lain there a while longer, trying to get back to the place she'd been, with a Galen she did not know, who in his curiosity over her body had not been shy.

Nor had she been. For when she'd dreamed it had been her kissing him, prising open his mouth as his hands roughly squeezed her breasts. And that morning Roula had tentatively done the same. Trying to blot out the sounds of a waking house and slip back to that place she'd almost found. Her curiosity had become less shy as she'd explored her body, thinking of his closed eyes and that mouth that rarely smiled tussling with hers.

'Galen...'

She had said his name as if summoning him, trying to get back to that place they had been, her hand creeping down, and she had felt for a moment that if she dared turn the key she might enter beyond...

'Roula!'

Her mother's second knock had hauled her back to reality. Soon to be a new reality. For it had been that very afternoon she'd returned from school and been informed that her husband had been chosen.

For a fleeting second her heart had soared. Galen was coming home!

'Your husband will be Dimitrios Drakos.'

Roula had forgotten what she'd glimpsed that morning. Her experience of sex had been so far removed from that distant half-dream that she'd flicked the memory off, like an unwelcome show on the television.

And now here she was, frigid in a warm bed in Athens.

All desire leeched from her.

Yet she'd had that kiss...

And she started working for Galen today.

There was no guilt, no regret, and certainly she was not worried to face him, for she knew their kiss was no doubt nothing but a distant memory to Galen. A brief pleasure to him, like a glass of wine he had drunk—tasted and then forgotten.

She chose a brown dress with yellow squiggles and a matching fabric belt, as well as her brown shoes, but could not be bothered to pin up her hair, so just tied it back.

Then she checked her bag.

Four new pens: two blue, one black, one red.

A pencil.

Another new notebook.

And now she held the phone with so many contacts, and he must have diverted his calls because it lit up as she neared the square.

'Kalimera...' Roula said, as she ordered his coffee from the café and took her first call.

'I'm on my way,' said a voice.

'Who is this?' she asked.

'Joe.'

'Thank you, Joe. I'm Roula—'

He'd already rung off.

The doorman wasn't particularly friendly either, as her name hadn't been added to his list. 'I was with Kristina before she was unwell on Friday,' Roula attempted to explain. 'I'll be working for Galen.'

Reluctantly the doorman relented and waved her in.

Then her bag was checked.

Goodness!

By the time she reached Galen's office Roula had few expectations. Apart from the screens it was all in darkness, and she placed his coffee down quietly.

* * *

Reluctantly, Galen noticed.

He caught a feminine scent wading through the stale air of his office and despite himself looked up.

'Kalimera,' he said.

What a difference a weekend makes in Roula time, Galen thought. For her hair was loosely tied back and its colour displayed, but—and he thanked God for small mercies—her dress was appalling.

'Kalimera,' Roula said.

And to be polite—it was her first day after all—Galen did not look back to the screen. 'How are things?'

'Wonderful. I had lunch with Leo on Saturday, and I went to mass— Oh!' She realised he was talking about work. 'Joe is on his way.'

'Good. I'm going to have a quick shower.'

Galen headed through one of many glass doors and she grabbed a trash bag and, just as she would have done in her old job if she'd found a suite in chaos, started a massive tidy-up.

She was collecting coffee cups, wrappers, when Galen's voice startled her. 'The cleaning team does that.'

'I'm sure,' Roula said. 'I was just...'

'Please don't.'

'It's habit.'

'Perhaps.' Galen nodded. 'But I like things left as they are.'

'Okay.'

His scent cut the air now. Citrussy. And he must have shaved in the shower, Roula thought, because he had been gone just a few scant minutes and returned, clean shaven, wearing fresh dark jeans and a thin grey jumper that was a little damp on the shoulder.

Perhaps from his wet hair, or maybe he really hadn't dried off.

Well, not to Roula's exacting standards.

Actually, she did not have exacting standards about men drying their shoulders except where Galen was concerned, and the blush that had stayed down on her first glimpse since that kiss emerged a little now.

'All okay?' Galen asked.

'Yes.' Roula nodded.

'We're not awkward?' he checked.

'No,' Roula said, and she gave him a smile. 'Not awkward at all. I've had ten kisses since then...'

Galen smiled at her little joke.

He wanted to add, *I haven't.*

Nada.

In fact, since Costa had informed him about a certain wedding on Anapliró there'd been nothing.

Save for one kiss…

And, despite the state of his office, he had not got an awful lot of work done, either. Well, certainly not enough for Galen's obsessive standards.

He'd been cross with himself when he'd come back to the office late on Friday.

Then he'd been distracted by the prospect of her arrival on Monday.

And now he was distracted because she was here.

For there was that sunshine scent and those wavy patterns before his eyes.

Only it was not the patterns playing hell with his mind.

It was a very different type of sensory overload Galen was dealing with this Monday morning.

'I need to get on.'

'Of course.'

Roula happily gave up on his appalling office and found, to her surprise, that there was a gorgeous coffee machine. Yet he preferred his from the café?

There was also a fridge, piled high with flavoured sparkling caffeinated beverages. Her addiction of choice! And a whole jar of chocolate balls on the table—the ones with the liquid centre and others with pieces of praline.

She had to walk past ground control to get there, but Galen was always lost in his screens.

He was trying to be.

He breathed out and watched as she wandered over to the glass table and took another handful of chocolate balls.

Everyone did.

It was just what they did.

Yet now he was considering moving the glass jar because he was looking at her bottom—and, God, that was *not* Galen at work.

The whole lot of his staff could be naked and feeding each other chocolate balls and he'd barely glance up from the screen. Yet he was looking now at a brown and yellow wavy bottom and watching how she reached right down to the bottom of the jar to get the last of the praline balls...

She was everywhere.

Her scent, her voice, those clumpy shoes...

On Thursday she returned from lunch with an armful of flowers, to brighten up the 'glass factory', as she called it, downstairs.

'Roula!' he called. 'Get those flowers out from the ground floor now!'

'It's like a mortuary down there,' she said. 'They brighten it up.'

'The staff will be in the mortuary soon. It'll be like an ER. They're all on puffers and nasal sprays…'

And then, before she left, she dropped a meal delivery on his desk.

'Galen?'

He ignored her.

She was more than used to that in guest services—except he was not a guest and nor was she the bearer of discreet nuts and a cocktail.

'Galen?' she prompted again. 'Your meal.'

'Oh, yes…' He stirred and reached for the silver-wrapped food.

'Thank you!' she said rather sarcastically on her way out. And then, as she closed the glass door perhaps a little noisily behind her, instead of freezing on the spot at her own audacity Roula actually wanted to dance.

She was herself—or rather, Roula was glimpsing herself…whoever she was.

Saturday morning found Roula surfing the net for jobs and updating her CV. Then, of course, the care home called.

Again!

'Kupia Florakis had a very unsettled night. More nightmares. We want to discuss increasing her night sedation.'

'Well, I can't give permission for that,' Roula said. 'I'll come in.'

The old lady was smiling when Roula arrived. 'Kupia…' Roula took a seat. 'How are you?'

'Cold.'

'I bought *lipsopita*,' Roula said holding up a bag, 'I need to stop, but honestly…' She could not resist the Athenian bakeries and cafés, and today was indulging in little buns with orange zest.

'That's good,' said Kupia and, teeth or no teeth, she certainly liked the bun!

'You had bad dreams last night?' asked Roula.

'No.'

She shook her head and asked Roula to hand her a photo, and as she took the frame down Roula felt a lump in her throat. It was a smiling baby Galen with his parents. Gosh, he was the image of his father. Well, a decade younger perhaps.

'Too old for her,' Kupia said. 'I said it would come to no good.'

'They look happy.'

His mother had been black-haired and black-eyed and in the photo she wore a simple white top and a gold cross. Her eyes were shining as she looked at her son.

'Galen's smiling,' she said.

'No.' Kupia denied it. 'He put soap in his eyes once, pretending to cry...he has no feelings.'

'Kupia Florakis...' Roula stopped herself. Oh, it must be so hard for Galen to hear this. 'Your daughter was very beautiful.'

'Yes.' And then she pointed to Galen and smiled. 'Cheeky boy. Talk, talk talk...'

'Did he?'

'*Why? Why? Why?* Every minute...'

They chatted a while, but after that it was mainly nonsensical, although Kupia was smiling when Roula left. And, no, there was no need to disturb Galen with the staff's sedation request.

Roula found herself outside a boutique so exclusive it had only one item in the window. It was a pale blue linen shift dress with a red flower on one hip, and this was the first time Roula's gaze had lingered so.

Her clothes, her hair, her absolute desire to be invisible had worked in Anapliró. It had been expected of her, even. But here Roula did not blend in. She ventured inside, but before an assistant could even approach Roula turned and walked out.

Then there was a hair salon that caught her

eye—though not like the one at home, where her mother went…where everyone went.

Of course she could not afford the one at the retreat. But here she wanted to be brave, and walk in, find how to tame her thick curls and…

Stop hiding.

Be seen.

She felt seen by Galen.

'I was wondering…' She looked at the hairdresser, a woman about the same age as she. 'My hair is so curly…'

'We'll cut it dry and then wash it.'

'Just cut it a little,' Roula warned.

She took loads off, and she sat there in silent horror as her hair fell to the floor. And then she lay head back and closed her eyes at the sink, wishing she'd never set foot in the place.

'Better?' The hairdresser smiled as Roula returned from having her hair washed.

No, it wasn't.

In fact the day got worse. Because her phone buzzed then—or rather *his* phone.

I need a break

Roula frowned as she read it, and then a follow-up message came in.

Do you?

It would seem that someone called Pandora would like to 'catch up' and was wondering if Galen would like to do the same.

God, she wanted to text Galen and tell him that he was supposed to be working! Actually, she wanted to message him about his *yaya*. But she swallowed it down and was a dutiful PA and messaged Pandora back.

PA

Roula even got a reply.

Whoops, sorry!

Pandora had even added a little crying/laughing face!

'That's better,' the hairdresser said.

And, expecting the worst, Roula looked up. To her surprise it *was* better. It was still almost as long, except it was no longer one vast triangle. There were ringlets and curls, and she felt glossy as she stepped back out on to the street, and kept looking in shop windows at her new hair.

Nobody noticed at work.

Well, she was busy taking calls.

Joe was cancelling, the care home was impatient...

There were so many she actually had to warm Galen's coffee up in the staff coffee lounge.

Galen gave her not so much as a glance as she placed his coffee down.

'*Kalimera,*' Roula said, and broke the silent Monday morning rule.

He didn't respond.

Because, yes, he had noticed—not her hair yet, but even her presence in the building was invading his peace, and now her scent was back, and he was so behind he *needed* to get on.

Yet he looked up, red-eyed and unshaven, and there she stood in a calf-length polka dot dress, with a matching belt and those Medusa curls...

'What?'

'Surly' would best describe his tone, she thought.

'The care home called, looking to increase Kupia Florakis's sedation.'

He glanced up. 'You didn't authorise a change to her treatment regime?'

'Of course not.' Roula frowned. 'I told them they'd need to discuss that with you—though she seemed fine when I saw her.'

'You went over?'

'Just to check for myself.' Roula nodded. 'We had coffee.' Really, it had been just a fifteen-minute visit. 'Oh, and Pandora messaged...' She said it as lightly as she could.

'Yes.'

'I let her know that the message had come to me by mistake...'

'Pandora told me.'

Galen turned back to his screen, when he would have liked to pull her around his desk and onto his knee. He wanted to kiss away that scowl he was certain was there behind the plastic smile as he told her that he'd declined Pandora.

He reached for antacid rather than the coffee.

This really wasn't working.

'Oh,' she added on her way out, 'you've got Hector at ten.'

'No, no...' Galen said. 'Not on Monday...'

'I know—but he felt terrible that he'd been held up on the plane, and given that Joe has cancelled...'

'Joe is head of my development team,' Galen said through gritted teeth. 'Joe is working his ass off right now...' He held his breath.

'Oh, God!' Roula screwed her eyes closed as she realised her error. 'I got the gaming stuff mixed up; I'll cancel Hector now.'

'Just leave it as is.'

'Hector!' She greeted him warmly and took him up to the visitors' lounge. 'Please, take a seat, Galen shouldn't be too long.'

She was lying.

He'd be ages.

And the trouble with glass offices... Well, Hector kept looking over at her.

Channel Kristina, Roula decided, understanding now why Kristina preferred visitors to wait downstairs.

'Galen...' She stood at the door to his office. 'Hector's getting restless.'

'Roula,' said Galen. '*He* demanded this meeting. I told him I had not got the time...'

'But he's here now,' Roula said. 'You'll feel better when it's done and not hanging over you.'

'*You're* hanging over me, Roula,' Galen said.

And then he stood up and walked into a meeting he didn't want to go to, with his PA who sat there like an umpire at a tennis match.

He was too aware of her, Galen knew.

Too aware of that jack-in-the-box hair that might uncoil at any moment, and too aware of the way she laughed when Hector made a little joke.

'Yes, the third game is the charm, ho-ho-ho...'

'My nieces love those charms.' Roula nodded.

'What we're trying to gauge,' Hector said, 'is the progress on game number four?'

Galen was silent.

'I'm aware we agreed on next year, but we're nearly halfway through this one…'

Silence.

Roula took a drink of water. He could see her out of the corner of his eye.

'Ideally,' Hector pushed, 'we'd like to announce a launch date at the ball…'

More silence.

It was not because he was playing hardball. Just that Galen liked to work in a vacuum—a silent, blacked-out vacuum—and if Hector got so much as a sniff that he was close, that in fact it was for the most part done, the hell of it all would start up.

Galen had done this three times before and he was determinedly putting off number four. Except he could feel, not just Hector's but Roula's eyes upon him, demanding that he elaborate.

'I mean,' Hector persisted, 'just some idea as to where you are…'

Galen spread his hands.

And now it wasn't silence filling the room—it was the sound of Roula's breathing. And he was too aware when she took another sip of water and pushed that crazy, amazing hair back from her face.

He could *feel* her frustration.

Certainly he was aware of his own—and it had nothing to with work.

'I said the game would be completed this year,' Galen finally responded. 'There are still several months left, I believe.'

'There are.'

'Then I'm still on time.'

It was all handshakes and smiles—well, between Roula and Hector—but she was breathing hard as she packed up.

'What?' Galen demanded.

'Nothing.' She looked up then. 'Just that the game's practically finished.'

'Oh, you know that, do you?'

'Nico said...'

'Your new friend?'

'Yes.'

'You have no idea of the circus that will start the moment I give a completion date.'

'Just get it over with,' Roula said.

'I don't need career advice, Roula, and I don't need you staring me down in a meeting.'

'I wasn't...'

'I was waiting for a kick under the table to prompt me,' Galen said—because that was exactly how it had felt. 'And, while we're discussing things, I don't need you to bring me coffee and pastries and then hover until I say thank you...'

'I just want to be sure you know it's there,' Roula said. 'So that you don't spill it.'

'No!' He would not have that. 'You stand there and...' *Make me notice you!*

They were having a row, Roula realised. Only it wasn't the type of row she was used to. Oh, she'd had rows at work at the retreat, and she'd dealt with them. And, of course, there had been rows with Dimitrios. But this in no way compared.

This was not personal, but it was not work.

It was the first exchange of words with a man that Roula had found exhilarating. Not scary, nor intimidating. It was not at a level she was trying desperately to ignore, and so she fumbled on.

'I apologise for messing up with Hector,' Roula said.

'This isn't about Hector...'

His hazel eyes were like two infernos, yet she still wanted to step into their fire.

'I'm going out,' Galen snapped. 'No calls.'

She stood breathless after he had gone, unsure of the energy that still swirled in the room, and then she tried to locate her phone, that was buzzing in her bag.

Or was it Galen's phone?

'Hello...?' she croaked.

'Roula.'

One word—that was all it took for the balls to clatter down. Roula briefly wondered if detectives went to voice training school, because she knew who it was even before she confirmed her full name...

And as for her own voice—well, she thanked the detective for letting her know in a voice that sounded oddly normal.

'Thank you,' she said again, and then somehow made her way on shaky legs and to take a call from her mother.

'The police are all over Nemo's...' Mamá was frantic, breathless. 'Roula, I don't know what's going on.'

Roula swallowed.

'There's a car outside!' she cried out, and Roula could picture her, peering out of the window. 'The police are coming to the door. What the hell is going on?'

'Mamá...' Roula attempted, but was saved from answering as presumably her mother opened the door and those deep detective voices were there in the background.

'Kupia Kyrios?'

The phone went silent.

CHAPTER NINE

'WHERE'S ROULA?' ASKED GALEN, frowning, when he returned from his walk.

Dora shrugged.

He guessed she was at lunch—though it didn't really matter. Well, it *shouldn't* really matter. His staff were not chained to their desks, and there were a million places she could be, but he wanted to discuss the morning's events.

Calmly.

He wanted to reset the tone.

Have sex?

Seriously, for the first time he was actually willing to sleep with someone he worked with just get it out of the way.

Hate me in the morning, Roula!

Oh, and she would—because he wasn't her husband—but then perhaps they could get on.

He took another swig of antacid.

No…

He met with Joe, and with Nico too, and then just sat there. At least without her there he could work in peace.

It was an empty peace, though.

So he called out for a delivery of *bougatsa*—a sweet custard in pastry. Not because he was hungry, more because…

Only it was a silent delivery—from Dora.

'Where's Roula?' Galen checked, when usually he didn't even look up.

'She took the day...' Dora said, and went to leave him to it.

'Took the day?' He frowned.

'Galen, don't worry about it.'

'What's going on?'

'She has some family issues,' Dora said. 'You just get on.'

Dora closed the door on her way out, and in that moment Galen loathed his carefully structured life, and his absence from the world. He'd so carefully crafted it, but as he scrolled through the news on his phone he felt as if he'd been smacked over the head with a cricket bat.

Roula's life had fallen apart, and no one had thought to tell him.

It was odd to sit in her office and take calls.

Costa: 'How is she?'

Leo: 'Oh, tell darling Roula to call me, please...'

Yolanda, in tears: 'I knew something was wrong.'

Just an endless stream of people, and he was curt, or vague, or polite if it was called for.

Galen still had the news on, watching the updates and gleaning facts from the little they told and combining them with the bits he knew.

And then there was another phone call.

Her mother.

'I need to speak with my daughter…'

'Roula is not in the office today,' Galen said, as if he was the receptionist.

'Then I need her home number.'

'I'm sorry. I don't have it.'

'But she's not taking my calls.'

She wasn't taking Galen's either.

'What?' Roula asked as he buzzed the intercom.

'It's me.'

'If you're here to fire me, just say so.'

'Fire you? Roula, just let me in.'

She buzzed him through and he found her in striped pink pyjamas, with a lot of curls and ringlets. Her hair was down for the first time.

How inappropriate of him to be turned on, Galen thought.

'I just wanted to check in,' he said. 'I heard.'

'Yes…' She gestured to the television that was on. 'So has everyone.'

'I'm so sorry, Roula.'

'Well, don't be. I've been expecting this. I know I should have told you, but…' She shook her head. 'I thought I might get through the next few weeks before…' She gestured again to the screen.

Christ, Galen thought, they had a helicopter over Anapliró. And there were reporters both there and in Athens, where it would seem her brother was in custody.

'Nemo's house,' Roula said as a picture of it came on the screen. 'I found Dimitrios's gas cylinder in the garage. They haven't said that yet…'

'Okay…' He had to remember he wasn't supposed to know. 'Your mother called a short while ago.'

'I just tried to call her.' Roula nodded. 'I think she's giving her statement.' She shot him a look. 'She doesn't know yet I was the one who went to the police. She'll never forgive me.'

'You don't know that.'

'We *both* know that, Galen.'

'If he killed your husband, you have every right to hate—'

'Shut up!' Roula put her hands over her ears.

He was so bad at this type of thing…

'Turn it off, Roula,' Galen suggested.

But still she stood and, no, she was not feeling as together as she had first thought.

'I want to see my little cottage.' Oh, she really was starting to lose it. 'I want to see what they say.'

'Roula…' Galen took her arms and held them firmly.

It was a move that might honestly have spun her, only she felt secure rather than confined.

'Stop,' he said.

'It's my life.'

'I know it is,' he said, and it felt as if his two hands were the only things holding her in place on this earth right now.

'I thought I was prepared.'

'I know.'

'You don't know…' No one did.

'Listen to me,' Galen told her. 'We're going to my place.'

'No.'

'Yes,' he insisted.

'Hiding won't help.'

'For a little while it might. I can police your phone and we can lie and watch movies.'

'They'll be screaming for me…finding out it was me who informed on my brother…and you want to watch a movie?'

'Yes,' he said. 'That's what I do every year on the anniversary of my parents' death.'

He shared so little, and suddenly he was giving her so much.

'I black out my apartment and watch movies and I wait for the clock to move past…'

'All that day?'

'All the moments of a day I can't even remember.' He was still holding her arms. 'Pause with me,' Galen said. 'Don't do this on your own.'

CHAPTER TEN

ROULA WAS STILL in her pyjamas as Galen drove beneath some vast building and pressed a lot of buttons to get them into an ancient elevator. And then they were going up, to a world that was so blacked out it was like walking in the dark.

'Here…'

He put on some lights and dimmed them, and she saw there were couches, and no doubt beautiful artwork and such things, but her eyes were fixed on a huge globe.

'Come on.' He took her arm. 'I'll show you around.'

'I don't need a tour.'

'Then nor do I.'

It was so dark she had to feel her way to find the sofa. It was vast, and just so nice to half sit, half lie in a silence broken only by their buzzing phones, which Galen checked now and then.

So dark that when she reached for her soda and drank it she pulled a face. 'What the hell…?'

'Antacid,' Galen said. 'Mia poisoned me.'

He'd made her smile, but then her face changed. 'Has she messaged?'

'Not yet,' Galen said. 'But Yolanda called, and Costa, Leo…'

'Can we please not talk about it?'

'Of course.'

He suggested a movie.

'You watch on a computer?' Roula frowned as he set up his laptop. 'I thought you'd be a bit more high-tech than that.'

'The screen's in my bedroom.'

'Galen!' She half laughed as she stood up. 'I'm not exactly dressed to kill…'

It was the biggest bed. They could have lain there like separate stars if they chose. But they sat propped up, and he rang out for food, and they watched the most dreadful movie, and she drank iced soda and Galen drank iced tea.

It was so nice *not* to talk about it—but of course the world was waiting for her, and despite the blacked-out room she knew it was getting late.

'I should have brought a toothbrush and things.'

'I have all that.' He wandered into his bathroom and came back to hand her a lovely little bag. 'I sometimes choose the lady's one when I fly. For guests…'

He must fly first class, because it was a gorgeous bag, crammed with beautiful things. But she was so tense she just grabbed the toothbrush, and as she brushed her teeth she made up her mind.

'I'm going to call my mother,' Roula said when she returned to the bedroom. 'She's surely finished giving her statement now?'

'Why don't I check your messages first?'

Roula nodded.

'I'm going to shower,' Galen said as he retrieved their phones. 'The guest rooms are down the hall, if you want. The second or third door.'

But as he went to the bathroom, rather than heading off, she sat on the bed.

She didn't want to be alone this night.

Yet she didn't want sex.

Or she sort of did—but not in disgusting night-wear, and unshaved, and just...

Oh, it might not be supposed to matter, but Roula had had enough sex where it *really* hadn't mattered. A very different thing. For a while it was perhaps nice to feel wanted, no matter your attire, but for Roula things were a little more complex. She had been taken over and over, no matter what she wore or how she looked.

She wanted to feel nice—not just for him, but herself.

'Still here?' Galen said when he came out of the shower, wrapped in a towel.

'Well, I want to hear what's being said. I assume you've checked my phone?'

'I have.' Galen nodded. 'Do you want to go through to the lounge for a debriefing and then I'll show you to a guest room, or do you want to speak here in bed?'

Why was he *so* direct?

'Here's fine, but...'

'Roula…' He opened and closed several drawers as he spoke 'I have a rule…'

'What?'

He tapped his ring finger. 'They don't turn me on.'

He did not see her burning cheeks, for he was still looking through drawers.

She diverted her eyes as he pulled on some dark grey lounge pants, which were tight at the bottom and had clearly never been worn because they had a price label on the front of the waistband—though she tried not to notice as he got under the sheets.

'Get in,' he said, and she did, and they faced each other, and his shoulders were broad and wet…

'You don't ever dry yourself properly,' she told him.

'I dry the important bits,' he said, and then added, 'I dry them very thoroughly. The rest…'

He liked her pink blush and the temporary receding of pain in her eyes.

It wouldn't last.

Galen had heard her mother's tirade, and it would seem that Nemo's lawyers, along with her family, were rather hoping Roula might want to fabricate a suitable defence and help Nemo.

Galen was not one for affection, but he would

have liked to wrap her up right now and hide her for six months. He was incredibly relieved that she lay in his bed, not down a hallway, or streets away, or on Anapliró...

He resisted, though. Even as he saw the trouble swirling in her eyes...

'Your mother did call, but I think you should wait till tomorrow to call her back. Tensions are high.'

'What did she say?'

'I was brushing my teeth,' he said, 'so I didn't get all the details. But anger was the general drift.'

'Did she call me a traitor?'

'Not sure... I was gargling.'

Galen breathed on her, and it was minty and antiseptic, and Roula had never imagined, not even in her wildest panics about what her mother would say, that it would even possible for it to be delivered in such an offhand, calm, minty and, yes, *sexy* way.

And as he went through her messages he took out, not the agony as such—this was too heavy for that—but he dulled the acute sting in a way she could not have envisaged.

'Can I ask how you're doing?' Galen asked her.

'Grateful to pause,' she admitted. 'So, you hide

yourself here on the anniversary of your parents' death…?'

He regretted telling her already. 'Yes.'

'You don't remember them?'

'I've always said I don't,' he admitted. 'But now, I'm not sure if it's all the photos I've seen, sometimes… I really don't like talking about it, Roula.'

'I don't enjoy talking about my murderous brother,' she said, 'yet here we are.'

Then she asked what his PA should not. 'You didn't take the flowers that I picked for your grandmother…'

'I'll send you to the guest room,' he joked. Sort of.

'Send me, then,' Roula said. 'Why can't you speak about her home to her?'

'I want to get this last bit right—for her to be peaceful. I've caused enough upset in her life…'

'I think her life gave her a lot of upsets other than just you.'

'Yes, but I was not an easy child. I wandered off…didn't speak till I was four…'

Roula frowned as she recalled some of what Yaya had said. *'Why? Why? Why?'*

She wasn't sure he was right.

'Galen, there weren't exactly a lot of specialists

available then—even until recently there wasn't a clinic. We were all fumbling along...'

'I was angry. She wanted me to love my parents, to kiss their photos, to cry, and I said they were strangers to me.' He gave her a grim smile at the admission.

'Well, I did everything I was told and now my family is not speaking to me.' She looked at him. 'Galen, she just wants to talk of home.'

'And I cannot stand it. Because she shouts and then she cries...'

'I know it's hard, but if you just listen to her it might help you both.'

'Thanks, Dr Roula. I'll let the specialist team know your recommendations.'

'Good!'

'I was being sarcastic.'

'I know you were, but I wasn't!' She took a breath. 'Galen—'

'My turn for questions now,' he interrupted.

'I told you—I don't want to talk about it,' Roula flared.

'See?'

But he moved his hand to much nicer distractions, up to her shoulder, and then a little question that had beguiled him when they'd kissed came to his mind again. 'There are a lot of straps...'

'Yes.'

'Two bras?' he questioned as he felt under her arm and then undid the top two buttons of her pyjamas.

Roula felt her throat constrict. It was with a delicious anticipatory pleasure and also a dash of embarrassment at her rather appalling underwear.

But he undid only the two buttons, and perhaps didn't even see the shabby grey. It was like a brief check, an observation, as if he might pop his head in and check all was okay…

Galen looked at the squash of her cleavage and then back to her dark brown eyes. She completely fascinated him.

He did up one of the buttons.

Just that.

'Are we crossing lines here, Galen?' Roula asked.

'A little,' Galen said as he ran a hand down her arm. 'Extenuating circumstances.'

'Yes…'

'But we're being good,' Galen said. 'Because we have to work together.'

'True.'

'As well as that…' his hand slid over her bottom '…you told me yourself—you're not like me.'

'When?'

'You know when. At the wedding…when I propositioned you.'

'I don't think it was quite that.'

'It was exactly that,' Galen said. 'I offered a one-night stand and you declined. Remember?'

Roula met his eyes and nodded.

'I want you,' he said. 'I think you are so hot, and so cold, and there are times I think you want me too, but…'

'But?'

'Okay…' Galen had come up with a couple of theories of his own—a few, in fact—and now he offered her one. 'Given you've waited this long since…' *Argh!* He couldn't even say his name. 'Well, perhaps you're holding on for someone who can give you more than sex. But that's all I give, Roula. I am terrible at relationships. I just don't do them—'

'Galen,' Roula cut in. 'I'm honestly not ready for one,' she admitted. 'I'm just not. But can I say this one thing?'

'Go ahead.'

'You *are* good at relationships. You have amazing friends, and not by chance, and I was wrong about your work—you have staff who are devoted to you. Again not by chance.'

'Perhaps,' Galen said, 'but I don't want an intimate relationship. I don't want to lie here and say the wrong thing, or ask, *Honey, how was your day?* and pretend to listen as I tune out. All that…' He shrugged. 'I tried all that when I was still going by the *Find the One and Settle Down* rule book. It never worked.'

'How?'

'First one?' Galen said. 'She asked where we were going—I said, "Back to bed, hopefully." You get the drift…'

'Second?' Roula smiled.

'That was a very big row. She asked what I was thinking in that moment, when we were lying there—you know…we'd just… And so I told her.'

'What *were* you thinking?'

'Well, Costa was wanting a cheaper office rental. We were really broke then, but the slightly more expensive one came with utilities included. I wanted to mine crypto…'

'Oh?'

'It takes a lot of electricity,' Galen explained. 'I was wondering how long I could get away with it before the landlord noticed.'

'That's what you were thinking?'

'Yes.' He nodded. 'After sex. When you're just supposed to…'

She stared back, nonplussed.

'You know,' Galen said. 'Float…'

Roula did not know that feeling.

'I ticked some things off your list while I was playing secretary today,' he went on.

'Like what?'

'I declined dressing like a charm for the gaming convention—so you don't have to run that one by me.'

'I was actually going to make an executive decision there and decline for you.'

Her hair had moved forward as she'd rolled over, and to Roula it just felt good when his hand pushed it out of her eyes.

'You smell nice,' she told him.

'So do you,' he lifted a strand of hair and inhaled it. 'Sunshine. But we're being good, because you're upset tonight and I am not taking advantage.'

He made it easy to breathe even with her racing heart. Always he reassured her—always.

Perhaps more to the point, there was no way she'd let anything happen. No flesh beneath her pyjamas would be touched or seen.

Roula was more than aware that she needed some kind of major intervention, but it was bliss just to lie talking. It was nice to just lie face-on and to really look at his beautiful eyes, to be locked away with Galen for a while.

'What else did my secretary do?' Roula asked.

'I got through quite a bit,' Galen said. 'One thing: "Ask about Pipéri?" What does that mean?'

'Dora's dog.'

'Oh?'

'He's having knee surgery tomorrow.'

'Seriously?'

'He's going to be on wheels...'

'Are you kidding?'

'No. Little wheels on his back legs, so that he can get around.' Roula nodded. 'I'd have done it for my dog...'

'Benji?'

Roula nodded.

'How did you know about Pipéri?' Galen asked.

'I asked. You should try it.'

He saw that tiny raising of her eyebrows. 'I do ask. I ask how she is... I ensure that I speak... And Kristina sorts out gifts...' Galen took a breath. 'Maybe you can send her flowers from me?'

'I'm on stress leave.' Roula smiled. 'Anyway, you don't know how his surgery went yet—perhaps you should call and ask her tomorrow?'

'Get out.'

Galen smiled, but he was staring, and Roula was back in another time in her life with Galen when a conversation was being had without words... when she could see he was thinking about what she'd just said.

But then his attention was back on her. 'I did something not on your list,' Galen said.

'Such as?'

'I spoke to Leo. I am your fairy godmother, Roula—you shall go to the ball.'

'No.' She shook her head.

'I thought a night out in a few weeks' time might be something to…' He rolled over and looked at her. 'Get dressed up…have fun?'

'I can't see it.'

'Of course you can't,' Galen said. 'But we'll dance, though we both hate it, and I'll mingle.' He rolled his eyes.

'I won't be working for you by then.'

'Exactly.' Galen smiled again. His hand was on her hip, and then he moved to her bottom. 'No more watching you pinch all the praline balls.'

She liked his hand there, just the ease of it. 'Galen, you said no sex.'

'We're not having sex,' Galen said. 'Just being a bit inappropriate.'

His palm was warm on her bottom and his fingers pressed a little into her flesh.

'That's all,' he told her.

His hand moved to her waist, beneath her pyjamas, and she liked his slow perusal. But there was vigilance still.

'Is that okay?' Galen checked.

'Yes,' Roula said, because she liked his hand

sliding over her waist, and then back to her candy-striped bottom, and she liked it that she wanted to move in closer, and that she could—if she so chose.

And she felt his circle widen a touch, so that her hip was just a little bare now, and it was so nice to cave in and hold his bare arm. No longer damp, but still cool from the shower, and so firm and yet silky.

'You're going to the ball,' he told her. 'When you no longer work for me. If you so choose.'

'Outside of work?' Roula said, unsure what this meant.

'Yes,' he said. 'No crossing lines then.'

'Oh, so we're talking about your "catch-up" list?' Roula asked, and it was actually so freeing to lie in bed and just talk about…well, sex, and a time when this would have all blown over, and they might know mutual desire.

'Nothing wrong with a catch-up list,' he told her.

'There's *so* much wrong with it.'

'No,' he refuted. 'Much like in my professional life, I focus on the things I can do.'

'And outsource the rest?'

'Pretty much.' He nodded. 'Insource, maybe,' Galen said and his hand slid up between her thighs.

It was so bizarre not to tense…just to feel

his hand move there and feel him cupping her through the fabric.

'Do you want to come a little to help you sleep?'

Galen spoke as if he were offering her a glass of wine or a couple of headache pills, and she stared back at him, a little stunned, for she'd never climaxed in her life.

'No,' Roula said. She did not want another first in her life.

'Okay.' He removed his hand. 'Get some sleep.'

Roula did.

A real sleep.

In fact she awoke with her head on her new and very favourite firm pillow, and she was not sure for a second which legs belonged to her, for they were knotted with Galen's, one of hers hooked high over his thighs. A little too high... He was holding her hand as if they were dancing, and then they both sleepily realised what had stirred them out of slumber.

His hand dropped and he moved her leg just a little, back down, and rearranged himself beneath those lounge pants. In fact, he must still really be more asleep than awake, for he picked up her hand again and drifted back off with soft snores.

And it was so nice that she did as her body wanted and just went straight back to sleep.

CHAPTER ELEVEN

GALEN WOKE AND turned on his phone as Roula coiled into him, and was stunned to see the time, for it was after eight. He unknotted himself from his bedfellow and then went out to his unused kitchen to check the messages…

Roula woke to see Galen sitting on the bed.

'Your mother remains keen to speak…' He must have read and heard all her messages.

'Who else?'

Her detective, her lawyer, members of the family, friends, her late husband's mother… It really was quite a list.

'I'm going to be busy.'

'We're in hiding, Roula,' Galen said, and climbed back into bed. With a groan, he checked his own messages.

'I might have a shower,' she said.

'Sure, help yourself. The bath is nice, but takes ages to fill. Do you want a shirt? There's underwear in the top drawer.'

'I'm not wearing your partners' leftovers, thank you.'

'I meant mine.' He gave her a smile. 'It'll probably be a bit big for you.'

Roula took the 'lady's' flight bag and padded

out to have a shower, but as she closed the bathroom door she blinked. Gosh, his en suite bathroom was stunning! Roula had only brushed her teeth and used the loo last night, and had not really been up to examining her surroundings.

Now, as she stripped off her pyjamas and her most appalling massive knickers, she looked up at the marble and columns. The subtle opulence was daunting. Seriously so.

Aside from the columns and such, two of the walls were mirrors—but certainly not the measure-and cut-kind.

Oh, my...

Roula stepped closer to one vast wall and saw the speckles and grey-green hue, and then she looked at the ornate frame. Of course she could not touch it, for it was saved from further damage by a thick layer of modern glass.

She spun and looked to the other wall.

It was a smaller mirror, though still vast. This one was unframed and had a crack running through it, and was so beyond beautiful it made her reach out.

Again it was set behind glass.

Roula looked at the beauty around her, and as she took off her first bra she felt shabby. For a very long time it hadn't mattered. In fact, the shabbier and more hidden the better she'd felt.

She unhooked the second bra and felt the drop

of her heavy breasts. She stared at the pale reflection of the large breasts she tucked and strapped away, and then looked down to her pale stomach, and lower, to the bright red curls that seemed too vibrant for someone who was dead inside.

Yet she did not feel so numb now.

She turned and looked at her bottom—the same bottom that Galen had stroked last night, through fabric—then back to her reflection. Roula lifted her arms and looked at the hair there—only it was not black and beautiful, like Galen's.

Unfortunately the lady's toiletries pack didn't come with a razor, so she looked at his razor, picked up the heavy metal, then stood under a deluge of warm water.

She could have been standing there a thousand or more years ago, Roula thought, being drenched by the rain. Except the rain was hot in Galen's world, and there were glass jars with bubbles and lovely fragrances and oils.

She shaved for the first time in for ever. Well, since her teenage days, and the eve of her wedding. And she borrowed his nail scissors too—though not for any practical reason! And she pinched some lotion and sniffed his deodorant, but replaced it unused. It smelt very male.

She felt not.

Roula pulled on her horrible pyjamas but left off the underwear. And as she bundled it, the she had when she'd wet her knickers all those years ago, something changed in her head.

She wanted pretty things.

And she wanted him.

Galen was not exactly husband material…

Bad comparison.

Well, not even relationship material…

Roula took a breath. If she was being honest, Galen didn't even tick the 'transition guy' or 'dating' box…

Yet Galen had turned something too awful to contemplate into something rather beautiful. And that languid moment when she'd briefly woken in the early hours… Well, Roula had gone back to sleep, but that moment rather fascinated her now.

There was a certain peace and harmony that came over her when she was with Galen.

He was on the bed when she stepped back into the room.

'I borrowed—' she started, but then saw he was on his phone.

Fine, he mouthed, and waved her away, thankfully oblivious to the transformation that had taken place.

Not so.

As Roula sat on the bed, combing her hair, he glanced over and tried—really tried—not to notice that her breasts had honestly doubled in size.

* * *

'I'm very pleased to hear that, Dora.'

Roula smiled as she combed her thick hair.

'I can't. I'm sorry. I have to keep it a pet-free space,' he said, and pulled a face at Roula. 'For allergies and such. But if you need a few days more at home...'

He spoke for two minutes more, then scowled at Roula as he turned off his phone. 'See what being nice does?' he accused. 'Now she wants to bring her dog on wheels in to work. I said no.'

'I heard.'

'Roula, I am not having dogs and babies and bring-your-pet-ferret-to-work days...'

'I get it!' She laughed. 'It's nice that you called, though. Send flowers.'

'Later.'

'What does—?' Roula stopped her question. She knew Galen did not speak about his staff, and certainly she wasn't about to dob Dora in.

'Go on,' he invited.

'Nothing.'

'Are you asking what does Dora with her lazy get-out-of-any-work ass do?'

'Galen!'

'I love her,' Galen said. 'Now, no one knows this—not Kristina, not anyone... Well, Nico does. But you can never tell.'

Good God, what was he about to tell her?

'Dora is my number one beta tester,' Galen said. 'Not that she knows it.'

'So you know she sits playing on games all day…?'

'Not all day.' He smiled. 'She checks her horoscope, does a little shopping, occasionally sends the annual leave sheets over to HR or stocks up the mini bar. But she gets through all the levels and we see the bugs, what bits she loves…'

Roula found she was laughing. On a day when her life was just crumbling she felt a surge of something new and she sat there and laughed.

'It's back…' Galen said as her laughter faded.

'What?'

'"Ha-ha, breath, ha-ha-ha, breath, ha-ha-ha-ha…"' He repeated the actual beats of her laugh. 'That's the laugh I remember. I haven't heard it in a long time.'

'Nor have I,' Roula said.

They looked right at each other then, and it wasn't the look he had given her at the wedding— it was a little more questioning than intense. Yet she knew so much more, and it felt almost as if his hand was cupping her down there, as she felt a stir in her body and an ache to step forward.

'I do want you,' she said.

'I'd be your first, since…?'

'Yes,' she said. 'You'd be my first.'

He must never know just how true her answer actually was, because she'd never really once made love.

But it was too much baggage—Roula knew that. Especially for a man who very deliberately avoided such a thing. And there would be ground rules.

'Roula, I won't change.'

'I don't want you to.'

'And I don't want to hurt you—I really don't. So I'm just making sure. What happens when I ignore you at work?' Galen checked.

'I shan't notice,' Roula said. 'I'll be too busy working, as well as applying for other jobs—though for the next few weeks you should do a better job of diverting your phone.'

'Fair enough,' Galen said. 'But I get to state my wants too...'

'Of course.'

'Take your ring off here, Roula.'

He would be the first person to see her without her wedding ring.

She stood and removed it, and as she dropped it on his dresser it felt as if she was dropping a lead weight rather than a sliver of gold.

Nervous, Roula went to take a step towards him, but Galen climbed out of the bed and walked over to her, and then he took her face in his hands and gave her a kiss such as she had never had.

It was not like the one he'd given her on the steps. This kiss was more silky than before, slower, and this one was leading to other places. She was lost in the bliss of his mouth, of his hands soft on her breasts, stroking her nipples and then cupping them.

And then he was pausing and stripping off his one garment.

Roula had seen him in a towel—had seen most of him—but she did not look down yet, just felt his beautiful shoulders and pulled at the little hairs on his chest as he undid the little buttons of her pyjama top.

'Thank God for zig-zags,' he whispered as he exposed her breasts, and then it was Roula who shed her shabby pyjamas, desperate to be free.

She closed her eyes as he took a nipple and sucked it to an indecent peak.

His skin was incredible, it was a relief to touch it, to hold on to his torso, but also not a relief, because it was too heady to be pulled into him, to be pressed against him as his fingers stroked her.

And then he stopped, half lifted her, and it was a kiss that dizzied her as he lay her down.

Now she saw him, and she lay there with Galen standing over her, and he looked at her and gave her a smile, and she looked up at him. At his jet-black hair and the thick length of him. And she was so burning for him that she frowned as he knelt and lifted her knees.

'What are you doing?' she asked, a little confused, a little breathless, a little awkward.

But his eyes were not holding hers, for they were trained *down there*.

'Looking at you,' Galen said. 'God, Roula…'

A part of her wanted to close her knees, unused to this, and yet there was something in his voice that made her tremble inside, and the light touch of his fingers had her curious for a little more of the feelings he evoked.

He swore, but gently and nicely. As if his own pleasure was somewhat inconvenient. As if he liked doing this—stroking the little knot she'd never even known was there.

Roula found she was tense with delicious conflict as he slid his fingers inside her. This strange push-pull feeling was consuming her, making her just a little dizzy as he stroked her, and then she was a touch bewildered as he lowered his head, because certainly her thighs had never been kissed before.

Nor licked.

And as his fingers slid inside her he kissed the most tender flesh of her upper thigh, and her bottom started to lift towards his hand.

She was caving in to the pleasure building—and then she sobbed in frustration when he removed that skilled hand.

'Galen…' Confusion reigned for a moment as he slid further down the bed. '*What* are you doing?'

'What do you think I'm doing?' Galen's words were dark with sensual torment, but he frowned slightly, as if he'd registered the note of bewilderment in her voice. 'Don't you like…?'

Roula felt as if her heart was lodged in her throat as she realised he was about to go down on her with his mouth. She'd had no idea such a thing actually existed. Well, perhaps she'd got some idea from a couple of TV shows, but she'd always flicked them off.

'Please…' Roula said, because she *wanted* the full Galen experience—honestly. She trusted him that much and he readily obliged. His fingers and his kisses had been enlightening, but his mouth made her feel as if she were chasing the eye of a storm. 'Galen…'

It was too much, and at the same time not enough. It was as if his mouth was attached to her, not leaving her, and then she was lifting up on her elbows, watching his dark head between her legs, hearing the desirous noises he made.

Or was that her?

He moved her legs over his shoulders and Roula had a sudden urge to laugh—but then he moaned into her.

One hand was under her bottom, the other pressing her stomach. It was Roula trying to lift her hips up, except he kept pushing them down, and she fought it a little, crying and red from the exertion of going nowhere except to bliss as he tasted her deeper.

Roula came against his mouth and it shocked her that she might—that she could.

'You taste amazing,' he said, licking his lips, and then he came up on the bed and sort of crawled up to her, rolling her to her side. They faced each other as they had last night. And there was a question she couldn't read in his eyes.

He took her hand. 'Stop biting them,' he said.

And then he moved her hand down and she closed her eyes, feeling his strength beneath her fingers.

'It's...' She felt the silky skin, and the power of him, and shot bewildered eyes up to his.

She didn't know what to do, Galen realised.

She felt him put his hand over hers and together they stroked him, and she was a mixture of desire and this deep pit of sadness, because she'd just never known anything like it before.

He was slippery in her hand and she let go, but then he moved down so that he was stroking himself, close to her.

'Please...' She was urgent. It was knotted desire and desperation, and there could be no halt in these proceedings.

They were side on, their legs scissored, knotted together as he slid in, and Roula closed her eyes as he filled her, so slowly she thought she might faint from the source of this pleasure.

'Never stop,' she said as she moved her hands up his chest and held his shoulders.

And he moved within her and she just watched him, felt him inside her, felt his heavy thigh over hers. Her hips started to move to meet his, in a motion that just came to her.

Then he moved, angled himself a little differently and drove deeper in.

'There,' she said.

'There?'

He pulled her hips closer till they were so locked together that her breath came out sharp with each measured thrust.

Galen had never been into a woman so much. He was watching her unravel before his eyes and resisting the urge to go faster, which was in such opposition to his own command to go slow. He was trying to hold on, but the intensity was beyond him and he started to thrust harder.

And she clung. And he caved.

His breathless shout as he shot into her was a mix of annoyance with himself and utter release.

To Roula it felt like permission.

She gave in to the place he'd led her, felt the throb of her body and the pulse of him, and so deep was the pleasure that the world lost colour, sound, as if her every sense had been diverted to capture every last beat of this.

They were breathless and still looking at each other as they came down. Still facing each other as she felt him slide onto her thigh. And then Roula found out what floating meant, because her thoughts were up in the air instead of reined in. And although she didn't want to, she started to cry. Not the squeezed-out tears of her first orgasm, but a cry for something else—her younger and other self.

Galen, who was more used to a smile, and zipping up, or lying in sated leisure before the next round, did not know quite what to do.

'Are you all right?' he asked, and hated his own wooden voice and his stupid choice of words after they'd just exploded together.

Even he had been taken aback by the intensity of their union.

'I'm just...' She wanted to tell him she'd never come before, never liked sex, hated it... But she was certain her truth would spoil things. 'It was amazing.'

'Maybe too good,' he said, as if he was cross with himself. 'I should have used something.'

'Something...?'

'Roula!' His eyes were wide. 'I swear, I always—'

'I know.'

She believed him, because she had been drowning in him, and actually it was she who was the practical one.

'I can't have babies,' she told him. 'So that takes care of that.'

'Good,' Galen said, and then winced. 'I mean, I'm sorry...'

'No, you're not!' Roula laughed, her tears receding, and lay there wrapped up in his arms feeling better, just feeling this gorgeous harmony. This was surely what Galen had meant about floating.

'What are you thinking?' Roula teased.

* * *

But Galen's mind was back there, hearing again the slight waver and question in her voice as to what he was doing before he'd gone down on her. And Roula's naivety… He did not like the conclusion he was coming to. Had already been forming the first time they'd danced.

'Charts,' Galen said.

Roula laughed.

Oh, God, he thought. How did she feel peaceful in this the worst of times?

CHAPTER TWELVE

THE REAL WORLD was waiting, of course.

There were hundreds of calls to be made, but the people she needed to speak to refused to take her call.

Roula left a message. 'Mamá, please call.'

She walked back into the bedroom, where Galen sat holding his phone.

'Costa called,' he added. 'I've told him you're fine.'

'You didn't tell him I was here?'

'Of course not,' Galen shook his head. 'I said you'd checked into a hotel and were sensibly keeping your phone off. I told you I am always discreet.'

'You did.' Roula took a breath. 'Galen, I don't want to take advantage, but I might need to take a couple of days off.'

'That's my plan.'

'I mean, I'm going to head home.'

Galen sharply looked up. 'You're going back?'

'Yes,' Roula said. 'By the time I've called everybody it would have been easier to just...'

'Roula!'

He was appalled at the thought. Galen had heard

her messages and, no, the cauldron of Anapliró was so *not* the place she needed to be right now.

'The whole point of you being here—' He stopped abruptly.

'I get it,' she said. 'It was nice to hide for a night, but…'

She looked at him then, and frowned, because the very suave Galen, who was so upfront about so many things, looked uncomfortable as he got back to his phone.

'Well, I'm not sure it's the best idea.'

'What else did Costa say?' Roula asked.

'Not much.' Galen shrugged. 'He just wanted to check you were okay. He and Mary are heading back.'

'Honeymoon's over, then?' Roula said in a voice that held a question—and it was *not* in regard to Costa and Mary's marriage.

Galen would know that. He rarely slipped up and was clearly rather hoping Roula hadn't noticed, yet she had.

'I'm trying to find a florist for Dora,' he said.

Head down, Galen, Roula thought. As he had done all those years ago—only it was not bruises to his face he was hiding now.

She felt angry tears pricking her eyes and she swallowed them down—for, yes, this brief honeymoon, for want of a better word, was over. And she took a breath and spoke, as she would for any issue at work.

'You said the whole point of me being here...?' Roula checked. 'Did Costa ask you to employ me?'

'Sorry?'

'Galen.' She pulled the phone from his hands. 'Answer me.'

Her cheeks were pink, her eyes angry, and it was truth or lie time. Galen never broke a shared confidence, but he preferred honesty over lies.

'Yes,' he admitted. 'Costa spoke to me after the wedding.'

Her face lost all colour.

'He was concerned about what might happen, as was I.'

'Galen, we hadn't spoken for nearly two decades—don't play the white knight here. You didn't give a damn until Costa asked you to step in. If he hadn't asked you to hire me, then Nemo's arrest would have been something you skimmed through on the news.'

'No.'

'Yes,' she said. 'Absolutely yes. You cut off contact the day you left. This was nothing more than a favour to Costa.'

'I don't agree,' Galen refuted.

'I don't recall you sending flowers when Dimitrios died. I don't recall—'

'He was just some guy from home who died on a boat,' Galen snapped back. 'Boo-hoo.' He stopped himself from voicing his emerging thoughts on her husband. 'You're wrong, Roula, because, had I read this news I'd have been on your to-do list to call.'

'Rubbish!' She was furious. 'Do not move me around like a chess piece! You don't get to decide when I'm in trouble, or...'

Her anger was white-hot, and perhaps out of proportion. Irrational, even. But this hurt at a level he could not know. Where had White Knight Galen been when she'd really needed him? Where had her friend been then?

'My God, Galen!' She was close to shouting—close to telling him that this was nothing, *nothing* compared to what she'd endured. 'Don't you dare control my life. Don't you dare play God with my career.'

'Damn it, Roula...'

She had her phone out now and was calling for a taxi, or trying to. She was shaking with anger.

'Don't go like this.'

'Oh, I'm going.'

She was. Galen could see that.

Seriously, she was going to walk right out onto the street in pyjamas and in a rage.

He said the only thing he could think of. 'I'll drive you.'

Roula told him what he could do with that suggestion, and not politely. But he would not let her leave like this.

'I'm driving you. I will not talk. I will not ask to come in. I will apologise. In fact, I'll do that now. I am sorry. However...' Galen took a breath. 'You are in pyjamas, and I think it best that I see you safely back to your apartment.'

She looked down to her candy-striped pyjamas and bare feet and he saw a tiny flicker of logic occurring in her angry mind.

'Yes,' she said, 'but I don't accept your apology.'

It wasn't the gentlest end to their hideaway.

Galen kept to his word and said nothing as he drove her the short distance home, and Roula sat there, angry, embarrassed and hurting.

And conflicted.

The raw edges of her anger were receding, but instead of calm invading her there was a new and unfamiliar turbulence rattling her. His car glided through the streets, yet she felt as if there should be oxygen masks dropping down and bells pinging.

She'd never been so angry in front of someone. Never dared to be.

And certainly she had not expected to be driven home.

She felt more naked than she had in the shower.

Worse, she felt lower than shabby.

A fisherman's wife…

Galen turned at her mirthless laugh but said nothing until he was pulling the car in at the top of the lane.

'We're here.'

And really, thank goodness he'd driven her— because he silently handed her the apartment keys that she'd forgotten to bring.

'You forgot this too.' He handed her her wedding ring.

So she had!

'Obviously I shan't be coming back to work.' Roula's voice was shaky as she said what she had been practising on the drive.

Galen stared out through the windscreen and forced himself to keep his temporary vow of silence, but when he tried to take her angry clawed hand she would not allow it.

'If I could have a bit of time to sort out the apartment, I'll return the keys by the end of the week.'

'Don't do this,' Galen said.

'What? You want me back at my desk doing some cooked-up job, pretending I'm needed?'

'It isn't a cooked-up job, Roula. You know that. You just have friends who want to help. I told Costa that I didn't like the idea from the very start…' He gritted his jaw. 'Look, I don't know how many times I've tried to give you an opportunity to tell me about your brother.'

'When?'

'When I picked you up from the airport.'

'You walked me home.' The angry flush on her face leeched away. 'That night when you asked what was on my mind…'

And she'd asked for his kiss.

She could not feel more humiliated.

'I'm going.'

'Roula, you can have the rest of the week off, but I expect you back at work on Monday.'

'Get lost!' she said.

'As a friend, you can use the apartment… I said that to Costa at the time. But I also warned him that I don't run a charity. I accept that you have some personal issues to deal with, so I will call in one of my regular temps to cover this weekend, but either you're back at work on Monday or you'll be replaced. Oh, and you have a gown fitting too.'

'You seriously expect me to go for a gown fitting?'

'Not if you don't intend to return to work,' Galen said. 'But if you are going to leave that window open, then don't go home till you've been measured. Leo is already cutting it fine to have it ready in four weeks.' He looked right at her. 'Unless, of course, you already have something suitable…'

She slammed the door and ran down the little lane in her pyjamas. Galen drove off, angry at himself, but at the same time glad the truth was out.

And worried.

As a friend would be, of course.

Roula stood in her lounge, breathless, and felt as if she had been running for ever—not just up the stairs to her apartment.

Her hand was holding the one he had reached for, but she let it go and tried to get back to her life, listening to the messages, reading the texts— and then the long-awaited call came from Mia.

'I don't know what to say,' Mia admitted.

'I know,' Roula agreed. 'I'm sorry for the pain your family are going through, Mia, but I couldn't tell you.'

'Of course not,' Mia said. 'But it's just back to square one, isn't it? Grieving for him all over again.'

Roula closed her eyes, for it felt a little as if she were being told how to feel—told that she should arrive back on Anapliró looking suitably widowed and ravaged to appease the Drakos family. Or defensive of her brother to appease her own.

Really, she would like to crawl into bed. Preferably Galen's. And just escape as he had allowed her to.

'Dimitrios's mother is bereft,' Mia said. 'I'm not sure what reception you'll get.' There was a long pause. 'Roula, I want to say it's fine, that we can be friends again, but I don't see how we can be. To be honest, I can't see me staying on at the retreat if you come back.'

Roula had learnt a lot from watching Galen, she realised, for instead of filling the gap she stayed silent.

'Do you know what I wish?' Mia said.

'What?'

'It sounds selfish, and I know you did the right thing, going to the police, but I wish you'd said nothing. I wish you'd just stayed quiet. It's all too big and too sordid, and I don't see how we can get past it.'

Roula felt a little ill.

'I mean it,' Mia insisted, even though Roula wasn't arguing. 'I wish you'd just kept your mouth shut.'

And therein lay the problem.

Not just with Nemo, but with all of it—it was the story of her life.

Stay quiet, Roula. Don't spoil a pretty picture with the truth.

Roula found her voice then. 'Mia, I'm sure you're not alone with your thoughts. In fact, I think most people would quietly agree with you—some things are best left unsaid.'

Roula ended the call.

Perhaps it was time to take a leaf from the *acceptable* rule book that everyone wished she'd abided by? To examine this with a more selfish slant? Roula thought, as Mia's words played over in her head.

She was better—so much better than she had once been. In fact, Roula knew she had moved on in leaps and bounds. Galen had introduced her to her body and shown her the beautiful side of sex. And career wise…well, it was exciting.

No more working on her past.

Healed.

Done.

Over.

On a day Roula knew she should be sorting out the drama of others, she was urgent in her need to deal with herself.

Urgent.

She pulled on a dress…any dress—she had an endless selection thanks to her mother's hand-me-downs—and put on shoes that made her slender legs look heavy. Then she picked up her purse and half walked, half ran through the Athens streets to Kolonaki Square.

Only she was not headed for work. Instead it was Leo Arati's studio she arrived at, and pressed and pressed on the bell, then realised she was too early.

'Roula!' Leo moved to embrace her. 'I've been calling. You poor darling… Come up. I've slotted you in.'

'No.' She stopped him. 'I don't just want a gown fitting, Leo. I want a make-over.'

'Fine,' he said, 'We'll do both. Galen has put you on his account.'

'Leo, I don't want designer clothes, or to be on Galen's account. I have my own money. I just want a friend to come shopping with me.'

'Shopping?' Leo gaped.

'Yes,' Roula said. 'I don't know where to start, Leo, and I don't know what I want…' Oh, yes, she did. 'I want to reinvent myself.'

'A new Roula?'

'Yes.'

A tougher Roula.

A more ruthless Roula.

One who allowed no one in!
There was just one teeny issue with her plans...
Roula loved Galen.
Always had.

CHAPTER THIRTEEN

FINALLY!

Galen woke in his temperature-controlled bedroom to a distinct lack of drama. He took coffee on the terrace and gazed not upon the stunning view but at his laptop, and the results of a couple of days' neglect, work-wise.

Well, a couple of weeks of neglect, really—things had not been running to his meticulous schedule since Costa had hauled him back to Anapliró for his wedding.

He *refused* to allow his mind to wander towards Roula.

So they'd had a row?

Certainly he was more than used to that with women.

Deliberately he didn't check the news—it was none of his business if she chose to go back to the island.

At least with Roula off until Monday, Dion, his regular temp, was due to commence work and order was about to be restored.

He went in and showered and shaved. To say he nicked himself shaving would have been a severe understatement, for his razor was beyond blunt.

Roula!

He looked like a teenager after his first meeting with a razor, Galen thought as he surveyed the dots of tissue over his jaw.

Oh, and it was a corporate day, so instead of his preferred jeans he pulled on a suit and tie.

He bought coffee on the walk to work and decided to get his visit with Yaya done early today.

'*Kalimera...*'

She was sitting up in bed, all rosy-cheeked from her latest blood transfusion and eagle-eyed. 'You cut yourself shaving?'

'Yes,' Galen said, 'thank you for noticing.'

'It looks like nail marks...' Yaya said.

'No, just a blunt razor.'

'As if she dragged her nails down your face.'

'I got you this...' He took out a bun and she chewed on it.

'Where's Roula?'

'I don't know.' He gave an impatient shrug. 'On some days off...'

'Did Roula do that?' Yaya asked dragging her fingers down her own cheek. 'Did you two fight?'

'What the hell do you think I get up to?' Galen said. 'No! Eat.'

Galen didn't stay for long, instead heading to the relative peace of work—except as he stepped in to greet those who were there it was as if a hundred screen flicked away from the news on Anapliró and they all pretended to get back to work.

'Morning, Galen!' Dora called as he walked past and then came dashing out. 'Thank you for calling about my dog. it meant so much…'

'That's fine.'

'It was unexpected.'

Well, it had been Roula's idea, but he enquired after the dog anyway, when really his mind was elsewhere, and found out that Dora's sister was staying for a few days.

'Good.' Galen said, trying to stop his eyes from crossing with boredom.

'Any updates on Roula?'

'Why would I know?' He knew he was a little defensive. 'I haven't even turned on the news this morning.'

Thankfully Dion arrived. He had no questions of personal nature, and didn't even blink at his slashed face as they went through his schedule for the remainder of the week.

'Meeting with Hector?' he said.

Galen frowned. 'Who arranged that?'

Dion pulled up the information. 'Dora.'

Galen rolled his eyes—and then recalled what he'd been in the middle of before he'd let the details about Costa slip. 'Flowers,' he said. 'I meant to send Dora flowers—not today, but over the weekend.'

'Sure. Saying what?'

'Best wishes for…' He shrugged. 'Whatever

her dog's name is—find that out. If it dies send sympathy ones.'

'Of course.'

'I'm really behind,' Galen admitted. 'It's been a disaster here of late.'

'Well, I'll let you get on.' Dion stood.

Ah, the efficiency of Dion. Perhaps not quite the absolute control that Kristina kept, and in all honesty Dion was a little bit…well, *pouty*, as he'd expected to be employed for the full six weeks that Kristina was away, but order was certainly being restored. And the programmers were all safe from Roula's endless pops of pollen.

Dion just placed down his food and coffee orders and completely understood that he was grateful for them. That when he was lost in work he didn't even notice they were there until his hand reached for an empty cup, or he found his drink was cold.

His cup was always full when required. Perfect.

Except, without Roula's little hovering, no matter how full and warm his cup, he felt empty.

And it was back to long silences at meetings, which should be running so much more smoothly now.

At the meeting with Hector he took notes on all the research and feedback that Hector relayed, and all his hopes for the next game.

'We really would like to make a formal announcement at the ball,' Hector persisted. 'There'll be a lot of press and industry representatives there.'

Silence. It wasn't as if Galen didn't know that already.

'So are we?'

'What?' Galen asked. 'Are *we* what?'

'Are you close?'

Dion was a consummate professional—so much so that Galen had actually forgotten that he was even in the meeting room—and there was silence…lovely silence. No little prompt from Roula. No feeling his ankle was about to be kicked under the table if he didn't give a timely response.

Yet, despite her absence, he could hear her voice.

'Just get it out of the way,' Roula had said, and had told him about her lists, and how good it felt to add a tick.

The game *was* actually ready—well, for the most part. But a million things had pinged in to distract him, and he really, seriously needed to focus on the work that was vital to him. And he didn't want to deal with the social side.

Yet, look at what Roula was dealing with right now…

Why did all roads lead there?

'Hector,' Galen said, 'you will be able to an-nounce a date by the ball.'

'Really?'

Even Dion looked up.

'Yes,' Galen said. 'There are a few glitches to iron out, but we're on them.'

And on Friday he met with the development team, and thanked the very efficient Dion, who would be taking his diverted calls all over the weekend.

'So *she's* back on Monday?' Dion pouted. 'The one with all the personal issues?'

'Yes,' Galen said, 'to the former. I would never discuss the latter.'

Dion flounced off, and although Galen still sat in his blacked-out world, it didn't feel the same. Yes, Dion would take all the calls from the care home, but... As much as he might have resisted her invasion, blocking out the world had felt a little safer to do, knowing Roula was fielding those calls...

Saturday he was productive. Sunday not so much.

He found himself checking the news instead of his charts and looking for updates on her—in Roula's words—'murderous brother'.

Nothing.

'Hey, Leo…' Galen called his friend, oh, so casual, when he never called anyone casually. 'How are you?'

'Hungover.'

'Oh?'

'Galen, you know I don't rise before midday—especially on a Sunday. What do you want?'

'Did…?' He halted, stopping himself from asking if Roula had kept her appointment—because Galen didn't snoop, nor delve into other people's lives. 'I just called to see how you are.'

Leo had already rung off.

Mondays were never his sunniest days, but Galen found himself awaiting the arrival of this one and wondering if his ultimatum had worked. If Roula would return.

It wasn't the scent of sunshine that cut the stale office air, though, instead it was Dora. And she seemed to have caught Roula's hovering habit when she brought in his morning coffee and thanked him profusely for the flowers.

Galen held in a tense breath and pushed out a smile. 'How is…?' *What is the dog's name?* 'How is your lovely dog?'

'He's doing very well.' Dora smiled, but still hovered. 'I thought Roula was supposed to be back today?'

He said nothing.

'She's not?' she asked.

'No,' Galen said. 'She's not.'

It was after nine when finally he addressed it—the first ever meeting for *everyone*—and they all gathered rapidly, agog for updates on the news they already knew.

'Roula is taking some more time off,' he said, when he knew he should just take her off the books. 'Also,' he added, 'Dora's dog continues to do well.'

'Should we send Roula some flowers?' Nico suggested. 'And a card?'

'And what do we write?' Galen fired back. '"Sorry to hear your brother killed your husband"?'

'We could just say that we're all thinking of her,' Dora suggested.

'No flowers,' Galen said. Because presumably her absence meant Roula was in Anapliró, and the thought made him feel ill.

Or was it his ulcer?

'How about chocolate?' someone else chimed in.

'Very well,' Galen said. 'Maybe send her a jar of praline balls.'

'No need…'

They all looked round at the sound of Roula's voice. 'But thank you for the thought.' She glanced over to Galen. 'I apologise for being late. I had a meeting this morning.'

'That's fine,' Galen said—it was all he could manage.

Far from fraught and ravaged, she looked sensational. Seriously so.

Roula wore a wrap-over dress dotted with red poppies with black velvet centres, tied at the hip with a red velvet bow. And shoes that were far better suited to her pretty feet than those brown ones.

Yet she still wore her wedding ring.

He would never know her. Galen was quite sure of that. Reading Braille would be easier—and that was not an idle thought, because he'd actually dabbled in it once.

'Roula!' Dora jumped up. 'We've all been so worried.'

'Honestly, I'm fine…'

She smiled a new smile—one he hadn't yet seen. For it was neither her PA smile, nor her guest services manager smile, just a bright, breezy smile that went absolutely nowhere—certainly not to her eyes.

'I knew this was coming. I'm just embarrassed at all the drama it's caused.'

He caught up with her a short while after, feeding paper into a shredder, and she looked up and gave him that smile.

'How are you?' Galen asked. 'Really?'

'I'm actually relieved.'

'Come off it, Roula. How has it been?'

'Fine,' she said. 'You were right—it was sensible of me not to go back to the island just yet. So I've dealt with most of it over the phone. I had a legal meeting this morning—that's why I was late.'

'That's it?' he checked.

'Pretty much.'

'I'll call Leo, then.' Galen shrugged. 'And get the gossipy version from him. And Costa's due back next week...'

'I thought you didn't chat about your staff?'

'I don't. But I do have a social life, and I'm sure we'll catch up soon, and they'll talk. I don't police the topics.'

'You just listen?'

'Yes.' Galen smiled. 'You learn a lot more that way. Look, do you want to go for dinner later and—?'

'No, thank you. I just want to get through these next few weeks as professionally as I can. I've put you down as a reference, as I've filled in a few job applications. I hope that's okay?'

'Of course.'

And Galen really *was* arrogant and aloof, because he went to walk off.

* * *

Despite her best intentions the new Roula couldn't quite leave it there.

'I'm glad I've made it all so convenient for you,' she called to his back, but instantly regretted her words. Because, watching his demeanour change, she knew her embarrassment had made her lash out in a way that wasn't fair.

Still, he quickly rallied.

'Convenient?' Galen checked. 'That's the last word I'd use to describe you.' He looked right at her. 'But do turn me into the bad guy here if it helps, Roula.'

'Meaning…?'

'Roula.' Galen was sharp. 'I have walked many people to their door, the lanes here don't always allow for car access, and…'

'And what?'

'I'm saying that if, say, I walked Dora or Kristina to their door and they asked me to kiss them…' He thought for a moment. 'Well, the answer would be no. And I can't even envisage a time I'd be lying in bed with either of them…' He gave a little shudder at the thought. 'I'm not a tap you can turn on and off. We had great sex and now, for whatever reason, you're regretting it.'

'I regret that you lied in the first place.'

'I've already apologised for that,' Galen said.

'But I'm not apologising for kissing you, nor for our having sex. I gave up self-flagellation a long time ago.'

'Along with your morals?'

'I'm not the one wearing a wedding ring,' Galen pointed out. 'I'm not the one feeling guilty because I happened to enjoy it.'

'Well, it won't be happening again.'

'Probably for the best,' Galen agreed. 'This Monday morning post-mortem kind of takes the shine off it a bit—even if it is a week late. Now, if you'll excuse me, I'd really like to get on with my work.'

Yet *still* he couldn't.

He had never second-guessed himself over sex but there he sat in his office, doing a Dora and pretending to work, but really he was just staring at the screen.

There was something wrong, something missing… It was a problem he could not solve, and for once it had nothing to do with numbers.

Kristina had had her baby—bang on her due date, of course—and it was Galen who told her.

'Hey, Roula.'

He came to her door wearing a really nice smile. He looked all scruffy in black, and up-all-night-looking, and she wanted to run to him.

'Yes, Galen?'

'Kristina just called,' he told her. 'The baby is here...'

'And?'

'Sorry...' He turned away. 'I thought you would like to know.'

God, had she changed so much that he thought she would give such a surly response to the news?

'Galen?' She called him back. 'I meant and is there more information?'

'Oh, mother and baby are well.'

It was like trying to get mustard from an empty jar.

'What did she have?'

'A boy. But we knew that.'

'I didn't.' Roula shook her head. 'Do you want me to get a gift?'

'No, she had a registry.'

God, she got things so wrong, and while the new Roula should not care, she ended up in his office after her lunch break.

'Take this in to Kristina.' She put the wrapped present down.

'Why?'

'Galen...'

'Okay.'

He was sulking—not just because he hated the thought of a visit to Kristina, but because that damn ring on Roula's finger was flashing like a beacon.

'What did I get her?'

'A cream cashmere blanket.'

'Didn't they have blue?'

'She'll love it.'

'Thanks.'

He stopped by her office later, just before she was due to head out.

'You were right,' Galen said. 'The blanket was a hit.'

'How was the baby?'

'All scrunched up,' Galen said. 'I think I offended Ruben. I held the baby and said he was like a whole little person, just condensed, and he said, actually, he was average height.'

Roula smiled.

'And they think he's a genius, and knows his own name already, but I tried calling him and he didn't even open his eyes.'

'What *is* his name?'

'Luka,' Galen said. 'Luka the genius.'

'Maybe he is.'

'I don't think you'd know at one day old. Apparently, my parents thought—' He stopped then, because Roula was back on her computer, and they didn't talk like that any more. 'I'll get on.'

'Sure.'

* * *

Galen never chased gossip, but for once he headed up to level two of the building purely in search of it, and dropped in on Costa.

'How was the honeymoon?' he asked.

'I told you—good.'

'What did you get up to?'

'Hill walking,' Costa said. 'How's Roula going?'

'Well, she doesn't really talk about it.'

'I meant work-wise?'

Galen could not do small talk. 'Costa, what's happening on Anapliró with the families?'

'Crazy guns at dawn stuff.'

'Such as?'

'Just toxic. I've only heard gossip around the retreat, but Mary went and got her hair done in the village—she said she'd find out a lot more that way… Anyway, the Drakos family want the cottage back. The Kyrios family say it's theirs. They've decided that Nemo did what he did to save Roula…'

'A bit extreme,' Galen said, tongue in cheek.

'Ah, but, Toto, we're not in Kansas any more. We're in Anapliró now.' Costa looked over. 'That's a *Wizard of Oz* joke…'

'Thank you,' Galen said sarcastically.

'Oh, and I'm going to be without a head chef if Roula comes back… Mia's threatening to resign.'

'Bitch.'

'Whoa!' Costa said, because that was not the Galen he knew. 'I guess you've had it all from this end...'

'No. I told you, Roula doesn't say much about it.'

That gnawing feeling was back in his gut and Galen didn't like it—not because it smacked too much of feeling, more because he was starting to be sure about her husband. It wasn't like an ulcer—just a plain old gut feeling that had been markedly absent in most of his life, but ever-present when it came to Roula...

'Mind you,' Costa continued, 'Mia might not want to push her own agenda too much.'

'Meaning?'

'Yolanda's looking to pull back. I'm going to be looking for a manager.'

'Roula?' Galen frowned, but then put up his hand. 'I don't want to know.'

God, another thing that would get him in trouble if they ever spoke again. Still, even though he was usually less than interested in gossip, Galen was here with a question in mind—and he hadn't asked it yet.

'What was he like?' Galen was rarely nosy, but he knew that Costa read people better than he did.

'Who?'

'The man who died?' Galen said. 'I can't really remember him—just that he was very popular...'

'You know the type.' Costa shrugged.

'No,' Galen said. 'You read people better than me.'

Costa thought back. 'I couldn't stand him,' he admitted.

'Yet he got on with everyone?'

'Yes, but he was a smiling assassin. You know the type. He's a saint now, though.'

CHAPTER FOURTEEN

'ROULA?'

They were sharing the glass elevator and Galen's citrussy scent was too much…too strong. Death by bergamot, Roula thought as she stared ahead.

'Just how many jobs have you applied for?' he asked.

'Quite a few.'

'I feel like a reference machine…'

'Sorry.' She grimaced. 'I honestly didn't think I'd get so many responses.'

'London?' he said as the lift paused between floors.

'It's an amazing job,' Roula said. 'But I seriously doubt I'll get it.'

'Well, I gave you a great reference.'

'Oh!' She flashed her new smile. 'That's nice to know, thanks.'

'I didn't want to,' Galen said. 'But apparently you're not allowed to do otherwise.'

And then there was a moment. An awkward one. Because Roula had called in sick the day before. Actually, she'd taken the red eye flight to London, and guiltily called to say she was sick from the airport.

'Are you okay?'

'I'm fine. Just a migraine.'

'I used to get migraines,' he said.

'Did you?'

'Really terrible ones,' Galen said, and she realised he knew she'd been lying. 'With an aura and everything.'

'Oh?'

'Thankfully, I don't get them now.'

'I'm pleased to hear that,' Roula said.

'Well, I was very concerned for you,' Galen said, 'Dora suggested flowers, but I said they might make you feel a bit nauseous.'

'Probably.'

'Roula, can I ask you a favour?'

'I *am* your PA.'

'Exactly,' Galen said. 'I wouldn't ask Kristina to do this, nor Dion, but Yaya isn't eating.'

'Oh...' Roula swallowed. 'Since when?'

'Well, she's eating a bit, but...' He was rarely uncomfortable, but she saw he was now. 'Could I ask...? I know this is beyond the scope of your contract, but she wants fava soup, and the chefs there don't make it the right way, apparently.'

'It's not a problem.'

'You're sure?'

'Of course,' Roula said. 'I can take some over tomorrow.'

'That would be great,' Galen said, relief evident in his voice. 'She'll eats for you.'

But then the moment was ruined as Roula turned a favour for a boss—or a long-ago friend, or whatever they were—into something far more personal.

'I divert her with conversation while she eats,' Roula said, and then she caved for the second time. 'Whereas you just try to divert her with food.'

'Don't worry about the soup,' Galen snapped. 'I'll make it myself.'

Good luck with that, Roula was tempted to call as he stalked off.

It was a taste of home, Roula thought that night as she unpacked the ingredients—and not just ones from the store.

She'd actually brought a packet of yellow split peas from home especially for Kupia Florakis, and she'd brought the dried mushroom powder from there too. It was a dish famous on Santorini, and also Anapliró, where the rich volcanic soil meant it could never be quite replicated.

Roula sniffed the fragrant garlicky air and found her mouth pooling with saliva. The scent was just too strong.

She walked out into the hallway but the scent followed her there, so she went into the bedroom and opened the window and breathed in the fresh air.

It was like having Covid in reverse. She'd suddenly *gained* a sense of smell.

Galen's scent...the soup...

Stop it, Roula told herself, even as she walked into the bathroom and stared at a box of tampons that had been there, unopened, since her arrival.

New job, Roula told herself. New city... Brother facing prison for murder. Family disowning her.

There were many reasons for her period being late.

Yet as the soup bubbled away so too did her emotions, and there were long-ago memories of Dimitrios's temper at the arrival of her period each month.

Of course it had got worse when Ella, already having two sons, had announced that she was pregnant with twins!

But then she remembered getting her period one particular month, when that little baby who never was had made her brave. Roula stood there recalling it—the moment of decision. How could she bring a baby into a world that even she didn't want to be in?

Oh, please, not now...

Thankfully Roula had the foresight to turn off the fava soup before she curled up on her bed and cried.

* * *

Galen wasn't having a great night either.

Of course he hadn't made it, but the chef at V's might well weep to see Galen actually wearing his special recipe fava soup.

'No!' Yaya had shouted as she'd flung it towards him.

'Shh…' Galen said now, trying to soothe her. 'Come on, take your pills.'

She spat them out, and for a woman of ninety she was very strong, because not even Galen and the one-on-one nurse were quick enough to stop her from pulling her IV out—and that was before the transfusion had even started.

'Leave me alone!' she shouted. 'Enough!'

'Yaya,' Galen said. 'You need it.'

'You never listen to me!' she yelled. 'I tried to help you and what did I get? Trouble. Every day you bring home trouble. Get out! Give me peace…'

CHAPTER FIFTEEN

'*KALIMERA*, DORA,' SAID ROULA as she joined her in the lift.

'You look amazing, Roula. Glowing.'

'Thank you.'

Dora followed as Roula put the soup in the fridge. 'I've found a new baker's...do you fancy going—?'

Roula cut off the attempt at friendship. 'I'd better get this to him.' She held up the vast coffee mug and made her way in.

'Hey.' Galen looked up as she placed it on the desk and got an eyeful of cleavage. 'Thanks for that.'

'I made the soup...'

'Thanks,' Galen said. 'And I mean that. I faked it and got some from V's, and I ended up wearing it...'

It was sort of unspoken that his *yaya* was getting worse.

'I have a meeting at the care home at five—maybe we could take it over then? We can find out if there are any treatment changes before I dive into lockdown tomorrow...'

'Sure.'

'Then I'm in Rome next week,' Galen said. 'Back Thursday night...'

It must be very, *very* hard for him to leave, Roula thought. And, really, what a wonderful grandson Kupia Florakis had.

'I can visit,' she said.

'Would you?'

'I go there at the weekends anyway. I'll make sure I go and have my coffee with her next week.'

'Thank you.'

Roula peered at him. 'You look dreadful.'

'Thank you,' he said again. 'You don't.' He gave her a thin smile. 'I should never have told you to wear zig-zags that night.'

'Galen!' She raised her eyebrows. 'Let's not talk about personal stuff at work.'

'Where else, then?' He shrugged. 'I just want you to know that I wasn't trying to keep you down.'

'I know that...' She gave him a smile, because it was nice of him to say that. And then she did a dangerous thing. 'You were hot for me. I got that.'

'Yes—and it wasn't convenient in the least.'

'Well, I'll be out of your hair soon.'

'Yes, London's calling,' Galen said. 'Well, they've called HR for document checks, at least.'

'I didn't think they'd move so fast.'

'Funny, that,' Galen said. 'I was just thinking the same about you.'

And though those moments between them were getting less, they still happened. And if it sounded as if she was counting them—well, in reality she was. Wrapping them up like precious jewels and storing them in the trunk labelled 'Galen' in her heart that had been there for ever.

'You used to practise your English on me...'

'Yes,' Roula said, and then it was Galen who took out one of those precious jewels she had stored away and unwrapped it right in front of her.

'"*Does this bus go to town, Mr Conductor?*"' Galen said, and they shared a little laugh at the thought of her ten-year-old self and that time long ago when they'd sat under a tree. A memory so precious to this very day.

'Roula, I know I lied to you...but was what I did so terrible?'

'No.'

'So why the big freeze?'

'There's no freeze.'

'Come off it.'

'I don't want to be on your catch-up list, Galen. Once was empowering—but no more than that.'

'I don't believe you.'

'Excuse me?'

'There's something you're not telling me.'

'I have no idea what you're talking about.'

'Really?' Galen checked. Because, if there wasn't something then we'd be at it now.'

'Now?'

'Yes,' Galen said, and he clicked off the lights, and the room was blacked out apart from the computer screens. 'Seriously, you'd be on my lap now.'

Yes, she wanted to say, *but if you touch me I'll fall apart in your arms, and I can't.*

'You're so full of it…' the new Roula said, and walked off.

They were both very bristly as they walked into the care home later.

'Can you please not mention to her that you're finishing at the end of next week?' Galen asked.

'Of course.'

'Galen!' a resident called.

'Sir.' He nodded, and then turned and gave Roula a little nod. 'Thanks for this. It's appreciated.'

'Kupia Florakis.' Roula gave her a wide smile and sat down. 'How are you?'

'Cold.'

She was very bright this afternoon—and hungry!

'Where's Galen?' she asked.

'He'll be in soon.'

'He's tired.'

Roula breathed in, because she'd been trying not to notice the dark rings under his eyes or the fact that he'd lost weight.

'Look at him here,' his *yaya* said as she slurped Roula's soup and laughed at a photo. 'He was so cheeky... Some days his *mamá* would say, "Galen is too bold."'

'Did she?'

'Oh, yes. His father was a professor,' Yaya said as she gulped down more soup. 'I was so cross... He was too old for her, but he did love her so.'

'Your daughter?'

'They were so happy.' She nodded and ran a finger over the photo, stopping at the little gold cross round her daughter's neck. 'I had to sell all the gold to buy books for Galen and for him to go to summer school.'

'I'm sure they would have approved.'

'I could never sell this, though.'

God, just talk to her Galen!

She wanted to drag him out of his meeting with the carers and bring him to her bedside. Because these were some beautiful memories his *yaya* had. Funny and kind and filled with so much love.

But, yes, it was tough at times to listen.

Galen would have loved to be dragged out of his meeting.

'So without the blood transfusions...' He stopped, because he knew the answer to that. 'We can try now she's calmer?'

'Yes.' The doctor nodded.

'But she gets distressed at the needle insertion,' Galen said. 'Even with the numbing gel.'

'Yes.'

It wasn't as clear-cut as he would like it to be.

He wanted to call Roula in, but that really would be pushing the limits of friendship, or even an occasional lover, or anything really.

And until now he had always preferred making decisions alone.

Walking back into his *yaya*'s room when he'd just signed off on her life was the oddest moment.

She wasn't frail, or visibly dying. Instead she was perky and sprightly and scoffing her food!

'You're eating!' Galen said as he came in. 'That's good.'

'Galen!' She beamed. 'Roula came to see me.'

'She ate it all.' Roula smiled and stood, then addressed Yaya. 'There's more in the fridge for you. I'll say goodnight, Kupia...'

'Kyrios?' Yaya suddenly said.

'Yes.' Roula nodded.

'Nemo...' she sneered.

'Yaya...' Galen tried quickly to intervene. 'Do you want some more soup?'

'Brute,' Yaya said, and then she turned her little currant eyes to Roula, as if seeing her for the first time. 'Roula Drakos?' she checked, and Galen saw, almost before it manifested itself, the flash of contempt in Yaya's eyes. *'Bástardos!'* Yaya shouted. 'That Dimitrios.'

Yikes, Galen thought. *Not so coherent after all. Or just very accurate...*

'Roula.' He tried to pull her away. 'She says stuff.'

'Pig!' Yaya shouted.

'Galen!' And it was Roula who lost it then as Yaya raged loudly on. 'She's right!'

And then he had it in stereo.

'Bástardos!' Roula said, with so much venom. 'Your *yaya* speaks an awful lot of truth if only you'd let her...' She shook her head as the nurse approached with sedation. 'She's fine,' Roula snapped. 'Just close the door if she's being too noisy for you.'

And then she took Kupia Florakis's hand.

She would do this.

For Galen.

As hard as it would be, she would sit there and let his *yaya* be heard.

'Nemo beat Galen...' Kupia Florakis wept. 'He would hide the bruises.'

'Yes,' Roula said. 'I know.'

'And your husband,' she sneered. 'Horrible

boy.' She raised a gnarled finger and jabbed it in the air. 'Little Benji…he kicked him down the street. I shouted at him. Every time I saw him I let him know. They called me *trelós*…' she shouted. 'But I know what I saw. No one believed me.'

'I do,' Roula said, but her voice was husky. And then she felt Galen's hand, warm on her shoulder. 'I believe you, Kupia.'

'Bástardos!'

'Yes,' Roula agreed. 'He really is. But listen. Nemo—he's in prison…' she saw Yaya's eyes widen '…and Dimitrios has a bigger judge to deal with.' She pointed skywards. 'So now they have to pay their dues.'

'I couldn't stop them…'

'No,' Roula agreed. 'But you did the best you could. Look at Galen now,' she said. 'Look at the lovely man you raised.'

And then she moved her shoulder to remove Galen's hand, because she couldn't do this any more, and she gave Kupia a hug and walked out on legs that were shaky, and found the restrooms and threw up…

But that was for Benji.

When she came out Galen was waiting, looking as grey as she felt.

'I'm going to get some air,' she said.

She sat on the steps outside and almost wished

she hadn't said anything, or that the nurse had come in with the sedation five minutes earlier. But, no, there was an odd relief that it was out in the open now.

With the one person she trusted to never tell.

'Go to her,' Roula said when he followed her out. 'Galen, it's not Anapliró disappearing that she's worried about—it's the memory of her daughter.'

'I can see that. But right now I'm more worried about you.'

'Please,' Roula said, 'she hasn't said anything I don't know. Well, I didn't know about Benji. But, yes, I'm quite sure he was capable of that. Go back in.'

'No, I want to listen to you now.'

'It's done,' Roula said. 'Galen, I know you keep your word…well, apart from that one time.'

'I don't regret telling you that,' Galen said. 'I just wish it hadn't come out in the way it did.'

'Galen, you can never speak of this to anyone.'

'I would never do that.'

'I'm not talking about respecting my privacy.'

'I get that it might change things for Nemo.'

'That was about money,' Roula said. 'No one knew about my marriage. They were both bad.'

'Yes.' He paused for a moment. 'You're not on your own, Roula.'

'Oh, I am in this,' she said.

'I know now…'

'You don't!' she refuted. 'You don't know anything about me or what it was like. I was eighteen and I had no idea. That night with you was the first time I'd ever actually made love.'

Galen sat there, and in his eyes she saw she'd confirmed what at some level he'd already known.

And then she shared details she'd never thought she would.

'I looked at that bed,' Roula told him. 'And every day I prayed that I'd never have to lie in it again. What does that make me?'

'Normal.'

'Culpable.' She saw him frown. 'I mean in court. If they questioned me…' She shivered in the warm night air. 'He's pleading guilty, though. I'm dreading it.'

'Of course.'

'I was planning to leave him,' she said. 'I didn't know how, or where I could go—there was no retreat then. I didn't have a job. It took me a long time to realise just how bad my marriage really was,' she went on. 'After he died, I mean. It was a lot easier to be a grieving widow than to deal with it all. I was just coming to the point when I'd decided to speak to someone—a counsellor or something—but then I found the gas cylinder and that window closed. I knew I couldn't reveal it to anyone.'

'Well, I'm glad that you've told me. Well, not *glad*. I wish you'd been able to tell me before we—'

'Please,' Roula sneered. 'You'd have run a mile.'

'I wouldn't have.'

'Or you'd have treated me like glass.' She was adamant. 'It was better for me that you didn't know. I *hate* it that you know!'

Galen sat silent.

'Can we never speak of this again?'

'If that's what you want. But if you ever—'

She shook her head. 'I won't.'

'Roula?'

'I mean it, Galen. I loathe what he did, and I hate it that you know, and I can't stand how you'll look at me now.'

'What?'

'Would that night have happened if you'd known what you do now?'

Galen took a breath, because so many times he said the wrong thing, and he knew that he could not get it wrong now. Not for his sake, or their sake, but for her sake and for the sake of the next sex she had.

Because in bed… Well, he'd paused for a moment and then thought about it later…

But did he tell her?

'Would you tell me to get on your lap now?' Roula demanded.

The old Galen would have said, *Settle down, Roula, we're outside the care home*—but he didn't know what to say now.

'It kind of takes the spontaneity away, doesn't it?' She looked at him, and for once he stayed silent. 'I want a new start,' the new Roula announced. 'I'm taking that job in London. I'm leaving next week.'

And then, as simply as that, she took off her wedding band. She didn't even toss it away with venom—just let it slip to the ground with a little clink and then watched it roll away.

'Dues paid,' Roula said. 'I'm going to go.'

'I'll walk you...'

'Galen.' She stood up and looked at him. 'I don't need you walking me home.'

'Maybe I'd like to,' Galen said. 'To tell you the truth, I wouldn't mind a drink.' He took a breath. 'Just to talk... I don't know.'

She gave a mirthless laugh. 'I don't need your carefully crafted words, Galen.'

'I might need—' He stopped. 'Whatever you want.'

Yaya was as docile as a lamb when he returned.

'What did they do to you today?' she asked and frowned when she saw his strained face.

'Who?'

'They hurt you?' she said.

'No.' Galen attempted a smile. 'Maybe...' he admitted. And he took the little scrawny hand, all covered in bruises from the drips and the medicine he'd insisted upon. 'They hurt someone I care about.'

'That's worse,' Yaya said. 'I would have taken ten beatings to spare you one.'

CHAPTER SIXTEEN

ROULA LAY ON her stomach and thought she had never wanted to call in sick so much in her life.

She was bitter with regret at telling Galen, and raw with shame. And, yes, she'd read all those self-help books, and, no, it wasn't her fault.

Her very soul felt tainted, though.

She closed her eyes when she thought of some of the more intimate details she'd shared.

Oh, she did not want to face Galen and witness the awkward dart of his eyes.

But then she remembered that, as of now, Galen would be boarding a flight and soon winging his way to Rome.

It was a relief, and yet not… In six short weeks she'd become accustomed to having Galen in her days, and after Friday she would not.

And so she climbed out of the lovely bed—second only to Galen's—and went into the bathroom. Through sheer will power alone she refused to cave in to the nausea.

Roula dressed in one of her new dresses—a linen dress chosen by Leo, in a gorgeous burnt orange—chose flat shoes today, and arrived just before eight.

'Good luck,' Dora said as she walked past. 'It's Monday.'

'He's here?' Roula was startled. 'But I thought he was in Rome.'

'Clearly,' said Galen. 'Given how late you are.'

'No.' Roula shook her head, blushing as she turned to face him. 'Actually, I'm five minutes early.'

'Oh, so we're on contract time now, are we?' he snapped.

God, he didn't even look at her—just turned on his heel and walked off. And for the hundredth time she regretted baring her soul.

'Don't take it personally,' Dora said, just as she had the first day.

However, it *was* personal this time. Roula was sure.

Not that she would let it show.

So she held her palms skywards as he stalked off and turned to Dora. 'What does "on contract time" even mean?'

'Don't worry—he told me off too.' Dora was affronted. 'I was just checking my horoscope before I started, and he saw and said, "Are you ever going to do some actual work?"'

'That was mean of him,' Roula said.

'I told him this place would fall apart without me,' Dora grumbled. 'Well, I didn't actually say that...'

Roula was trying not to smile. Galen actually had the patience of a saint where Dora was concerned. In fact, he'd created an entire job around her lack of commitment!

'It's his *yaya*…' Dora whispered.

'What?' Roula stepped in. 'Was she taken ill?'

'No…' Dora motioned for her to close the door. 'Apparently there was a meeting. I just heard him on the phone to Galilee, asking about a bed.'

Roula swallowed. Galilee was a palliative care home.

'I think he's actually going to keep her where she is, but you know Galen—there'll be a thousand second opinions before he makes up his mind.' Dora looked up then. 'Were you there?'

'Not at the meeting.' Roula shook her head. 'I was just dropping off some soup.'

'Well, that's all I know.' Dora gave a worried sigh. 'Poor Galen. From the sound of things, I don't think it will be very long.'

Oh, no…

Vividly she recalled him standing at the door, smiling, pleased to see that his grandmother had eaten, and then…

And then it had become all about *Roula, Roula, Roula.* Dealing with her stuff when there should surely have been a moment for his.

He'd asked her to go for a drink.

He had actually been asking to speak with her…

Damn!

'Galen?' She knocked on the open glass door. He didn't look up. 'I just heard about Yaya.'

'It's fine.'

'Clearly it's not. Galen, it never entered my head that you'd been through a difficult meeting. It should have...she's so frail. I just wasn't thinking straight.'

'Of course not.' He let out a breath. 'Nor was I.'

'They'd just told you?'

'No,' Galen said.

'I'm not with you...'

He relented a touch. 'I kind of told them.'

'Oh.' She waited for details, but none were forthcoming. 'What did you say?'

'Roula...' he was very direct '...we can't talk about you, correct?'

She nodded.

'Yet you feel we can talk about me?'

'I'm your PA.'

'Till Friday.'

'Galen—' she started.

'Save it for the sympathy card, Roula...' He glanced up. 'Airmail, I presume?'

The bite to his tone had her breath catching.

'When do you fly?' he asked.

'Monday.'

His phone buzzed then. 'If you'll excuse me? I need to take this.'

* * *

It wasn't a great week.

There was just a pall of sadness in the gleaming space—and him saying, no, he did not need more fava soup, nor any of her endless offers to bring in food.

Her last day was as flat as Kristina's had been.

Just a matter of tying up all the loose ends.

'Roula!' It was Dora at her door. 'Kristina's here.'

And for all Kristina's coldness there was so much kindness. For there was genius Luka, wearing the blue booties Dora had knitted and with a blue teddy given to him by someone else, everything blue, blue, blue...

'You look amazing,' Kristina said to Roula. 'I hear it's all gone very well.'

'Thank you.'

'No, thank *you* for agreeing to go to the ball. I thought I'd be able to go but, as I was just telling Galen, I can't be way from my breast pump for more than two hours. He said not to worry.'

It was funny to see the guys all blushing, and Kristina actually gave Dora a little wink as a few of them scuttled off.

'Wait!' Dora called them back. 'Kristina's here for another reason. Surprise!' she said to Roula.

'*You* get cake?' Kristina said.

And champagne, and cola, and even Galen made a brief appearance.

'Will you miss us?' Dora asked.

'Yes.' Roula smiled.

'We've still got the ball,' Nico reminded her, and Roula could feel Galen's eyes on her as she flushed.

They all ate cake, and then Galen asked if he could have a word with her before she left.

'Could you close the door?' he asked.

'Why?'

'It's all right. I'm not going to dim the lights…' Roula blushed.

'I want to talk to you in case I don't see you again. What I have to say has nothing to do with us.'

Roula closed the door.

'Sit down.'

She did.

'I might not be able to say the right thing, but Dora's a good friend to have—so stop shutting her out.'

'Pardon?'

'That's it,' Galen said. 'All I have to say on the matter. Thank you for everything you've done—and I do mean that. You've cheered the place up…well, for the most part. And, on a more personal note, you've been a great help to me and my grandmother. It's appreciated.'

'Thank you,' Roula said, and stood. 'I've really enjoyed my time.'

'Go.'

Oh, but she didn't want to.

Not just because of the Galen thing, but all of it.

But that was what they did here—a little wave... 'See you...' Only Roula couldn't do that.

'Can I ask you something?' Roula said. 'Your honest, unfiltered opinion...?'

'Are you sure you want it?'

'Yes,' Roula said. 'Am I making the most dreadful mistake?'

'Career-wise?' he checked.

She felt as if they were sitting under that tree sharing lunch, back to where he'd helped her with the bits she didn't understand.

'No.' He sounded honest. 'I think it's a great move. For all Yolanda's talk of semi-retiring, she'll never hand over the reins...'

'What about friendship-wise? Yaya, I mean.'

'Roula, I wouldn't ask Costa or Leo to cancel a lunch over Yaya. I hope they'll come to the funeral, but only if they're in Athens... So, no, you don't owe me anything friendship-wise.'

'Us-wise?'

'Us?' Galen checked. 'We had sex once... Had ouzo been involved it could have been twice...'

'Thanks,' she said. 'For being honest.'

'I haven't finished being honest yet,' Galen

said. 'Why now, Roula? Seriously?' he said. 'Why, when we were getting good, would you choose to go now?'

'You said you didn't want a relationship.'

'So did you,' Galen fired back. 'That was the deal we made. But then things changed. You told me some things that I don't believe you would drop into any casual conversation. You brought me right up close to here...' he jabbed at his chest. '...and then you told me you were on the next flight out.'

'It wasn't like that...'

'Pretty close.'

'I told you so that you'd open up too.'

'You're not that magnanimous,' Galen said, and Roula swallowed at his confrontational words. 'Deny it all you like, but we were getting close—and now you've decided to run.'

'Some things are just too big and too sordid to come back from.'

'Says who?' he challenged. 'Are you still reading from the *Book of Drakos*?'

'That's mean.'

'Yes,' Galen said. 'I can be. But so can you. Like it or not, I know you—or I did once. And before you tell me you can't make it to the ball, know this: I don't think *I'm* going to be able to make it. Believe it or not, it's work. I would like some notes made now Kristina cannot be there… And Leo has got quite a bit hanging on this bloody gown getting photographed, so just know that too, before you run off.'

'I'm not running off,' Roula said. 'I'm here, aren't I?'

'You haven't been here since you got out of my bed, Roula,' he accused. 'Now, will you be there tomorrow?'

Caught, she nodded.

'Good,' he said. 'I suggest you bring your Dictaphone. It says "no recording" on the invitation, but if you do it will be easier for you to write up your notes.'

'Anything else?'

'Not that I can think of,' Galen said. 'How about you?'

Roula shook her head, too petrified to share her unconfirmed fears. 'No.'

CHAPTER SEVENTEEN

'OH, MY GOODNESS...' Leo stepped back and admired not so much Roula as his new creation.

The gown was almost white, but not quite, and of the softest velvet with a halter neck. Roula didn't even recognise herself. The gown clung everywhere, and her hair was up so high that even her neck felt exposed, and as Leo and Deacon drove her to the offices in Kolonaki Square her teeth were chattering with nerves.

And she couldn't even have a glass of champagne.

'Roula!' The doorman smiled and in she went. Everyone looked stunning. Nico in a tux, Dora in floor-length silver... This ball was far bigger than she had envisaged.

It would seem Galen really was a no-show. But everyone was beautiful, and there was such a buzz in the air that she didn't even need Galen to feel excited for tonight.

She'd just prefer him to be there, that was all.

To think she'd nearly missed this, Roula thought as she stood with Dora and Nico and all the people who had been strangers to her just six weeks ago.

'Champagne?' Nico handed her a glass.

'No, no.' Roula smiled. 'I'm sticking to water for now. Maybe later.'

She had tampons in her bag, but then she thought of the dress she was wearing and it was odd… In the moment she hoped she *didn't* get her period tonight. She actually wasn't sure she wanted it after all. Or rather, she would be okay if it was nine months late.

Yes, she had a new job, and they wouldn't be thrilled, but look at Kristina…

And she had always lived frugally and had money saved.

It was odd to stand there and return to the absence of fear that she had found in Galen's arms.

To feel strong alone for the very first time.

To feel happy.

She smiled widely at Dora, who was chattering on.

'I said, maybe she's died!'

'Oh, sorry…' Roula wiped off her smile. 'My mind was miles away.'

'Well, the ball won't be the same without him,' Dora said. 'For all he's difficult, he's the best boss.'

'Yes…'

'Galen was the first person I told that I wasn't happy at home.'

Roula swallowed and thought about what Galen

had said about Dora, how he'd suggested they pair up.

'He helped me to leave.' Dora sighed. 'Anyway, I'm sure he's where he needs to be tonight.'

Galen wasn't.

He was all dressed up—well, for the most part—but Yaya would not let his hand go, and he did not know how to pull it away when finally they were speaking.

'I saw the *kandylakia*,' he told her. 'Candles still lit.'

She smiled.

'I put flowers there, and there were some other recent ones.'

'Where's Roula?' Yaya asked, as she often did.

'At a work function,' he said. 'And she heads off to London for her new job soon.'

'Hiding.'

'Not any more,' Galen said, and brushed the little strands of grey hair back. 'I tell you, once the shackles came off...' He gave her a smile. 'She's doing what she needs to.'

And he needed to see her before she went. Because yesterday's exchange had left such a bitter taste in his mouth.

Was it selfish to ask her to put her life on hold and be here for the next couple of weeks?

He'd hoped for more.

And offered her so little.

'I bought her a leaving gift,' Galen said.

He'd put more thought into this gift than he ever had before and was rather pleased with himself. It was an olive branch. A very expensive olive branch. He would take it to the office tomorrow.

'A nice one,' he added.

'Why would you do that?' Yaya sneered. 'Stupid boy. Go to your party.'

'It's not a party—it's work.'

'Go.'

He kissed her bony cheek and pulled the blanket up around her shoulders. Finally he felt that with Yaya he'd got things right.

He was late, but they were all meeting for a drink at the office, so he told his driver to take him there first.

Galen was nervous when things like this didn't faze him. He had lozenges from the doctor now, little minty squares of chalk, and he sucked on one as he saw that the cars were all outside. They hadn't left yet.

Would she even be there? he wondered, and then reminded himself, as he had to an awful lot these days, that this was work.

'We should keep in touch,' Roula said to Dora. 'I mean, if you want?'

'I'd like that.' Dora smiled. 'Maybe I'll come

to London. Do you think I could get a business trip out of him?'

'Probably!' Roula laughed.

'I think we have to move down to the cars,' Dora said. 'Oh, look—here's Galen.'

There was a lurch to Roula's heart as she turned around and Galen came dashing in. He was so stunning that it was hard to believe she had once been coiled around him, that his beautiful mouth had devoured hers. And elsewhere!

Her face flew to fire just at thinking about that.

'You look beautiful, Dora,' Galen said. 'Can you sort this?' He pulled out an arm and Dora started sorting his cufflinks.

Clearly he was late with sad reason.

'How is she?' she asked.

'Comfortable,' he said as he put on his tie. 'Hate these.'

Then he spoke to Nico and a few of the others as the cars waited to take them for the short drive to beautiful Syntagma Square, where the ball was being held.

And Roula looked on, a spectator now, until he saw her.

'Roula.' He came over and as always was polite. 'You look stunning.'

'Thank you.'

That was it. All those hours spent getting ready and he simply nodded, and complimented her just as he had Dora. Well, perhaps even a little less than he had Dora.

But it was not a night for sulking.

Even Nico seemed enthusiastic. 'I thought Roula might come with us in the second car,' he said.

'Roula will come with me,' Galen said. 'You are with the development team. I need Roula to go through my speech.'

They were already a little late, a little rushed, but they were all present and correct and it was their night of nights in a world she didn't know.

And she thought she would remember this for ever—how he rolled his eyes as they all argued about who was getting in what car.

'You want me to go through your speech?' she asked.

'No, I was just being helpful,' Galen said. 'You have a fan.'

'I know!' She blew out a breath. 'How old *is* Nico?'

'Nineteen.'

'God...'

Galen laughed, but it faded halfway and he closed his eyes for a brief second, as if he couldn't quite believe he'd got here.

'How is she?' she asked again.

'As I said, comfortable.' Galen nodded, and then she realised he was putting his game face on.

The passed the Hellenic Parliament and surely Athens was taunting her for leaving? For it was as if all the stops had been pulled out tonight. Everything was lit up as if to tell her to stay.

'Better than the school trip?' Galen asked.

'So much better,' Roula said, and wanted to add, *But only because you're here.* 'I lied,' she admitted. 'I have been to Athens before.'

'To see the police?'

She nodded. 'I did the right thing, didn't I?' she asked, because it might be the last chance she'd have to ask this man she trusted so very much. 'Going to the police?'

'Completely,' he said. 'I always said you were brave.'

'You did.' And it meant the world that he thought she was right—his opinion mattered very much.

Galen watched her look skywards in the little ritual she did when she was trying not to cry.

'No tears,' Galen said.

'Do you have a tissue?'

'No.' Galen said, but there were little serviettes for the drinks, and he passed her one of those. 'Yaya's in a good place,' he said gently. 'I owe that to you.'

'You don't.'

'Seriously, I've told them she's never been in a peaceful place in the thirty-five years I've known her, so they must stop sedating her.'

Roula laughed.

'She won't stop talking...' He squeezed her hand. 'So thank you for facilitating that.'

'I'm so glad.'

He looked at her then. 'You're allowed to leave, Roula.'

She wasn't sure that she wanted to, though.

'I'm sorry if I sulked about it,' he added. 'You don't deserve that. And now we're going to have a great night. We deserve that, yes?'

'Yes.'

'So let's do it.'

'Arati,' Roula said, whenever she was asked who had made her gown—just as Leo had told her to do.

'From his NYC collection?' they asked.

'I believe so,' Galen said, and named the colour on Leo's behalf. As they walked in, he said, 'Mist over the Aegean... That's what you remind me of tonight.'

It was the most beautiful thing anyone had ever said to her.

'You're famous here,' Roula said, as they stepped off the red carpet.

'In odd ways,' Galen agreed.

There were game charms on the tables, and Roula collected a few for her nephews and nieces. Even if the adults in the family weren't talking to her, she would send them with love.

'Red or white?' the waiter asked.

Galen declined. 'Not for me. I have to give a speech.' He looked at Roula.

'Nor me,' Roula said—and not just because of potential mini-Galens, but because really she was having great difficulty holding on to her emotions.

He hated these things, Roula knew—not that even she could tell, for now they were seated and he was laughing.

'No Kristina?' asked a guest wandering past.

'Not tonight,' Galen said.

'Oh, is she still on maternity leave?'

'Roula is my guest tonight,' Galen said.

No, he was not discussing Kristina and her pumping situation. God, he hated these things…

But then he took a breath and spoke to the man. 'Roula is from Anapliró…'

'Where the new game is based!'

'Loosely based,' Galen corrected, but he smiled. 'Do you know,' he told Roula when the man had drifted on, 'HR has informed me that I have to provide a room for Kristina?'

'For what?'

He glanced at her breasts. 'You know…'

'Oh.'

'And a fridge,' Galen said. Except he had lost his thread a little bit…because had Roula's breasts doubled in size again?

'You could put it next to the dogs-on-wheels room,' Roula said.

They both laughed, and it was the first time Galen had sat at one of these things and really laughed. Even while he was sad.

He remembered rest of the table. 'Dora, what do you think of the new version of the game?'

'I can't wait to try it,' Dora said.

Roula watched as Galen and Nico shared a small smile.

Aside from loving Galen, she adored them all. And, honestly, it was the best last night in Athens, with the most amazing, wonderful man, and if she didn't love him it would be perfect.

'Roula doesn't like fish,' he said as he swapped their dishes, and then he pulled a face. 'Actually, nor do I tonight.'

She had a creamy pasta dish, that was very nice. Dora didn't want the fish either, but it seemed Hector was happy to swap with her.

'You're quiet Galen,' Hector commented as Roula slipped off for some air.

'Hector…' Dora warned, and she must have given him a little kick, or said something, because Hector quickly stopped asking why Galen was quiet.

Only Roula knew it wasn't about Yaya…

'There you are.' Galen found her on a balcony, drinking in the delicious view. 'Speeches soon.'

'Coming.'

'We've got a few moments.'

'Yes.'

'So, London here you come?'

'Yes…a clean slate.'

'Your slate's already clean, Roula.' He looked at her then. 'If you do meet the perfect guy, will you tell him?'

She thought for a moment. 'No.'

And still Galen stood there, and he knew he could stay quiet, and perhaps that would be wise, but he preferred honesty.

'Roula,' he said. 'I already knew.'

She turned.

'I knew before you told Yaya. I knew there was something wrong when we danced—not the specifics, but…'

'You knew?'

'I don't delve into people's sex lives. I don't care if someone here's slept with half the ballroom. But after we danced I knew you'd been hurt, and then when we made love… I hoped I was wrong, but…' He took her hand and he pressed it not on

his chest but high on his stomach. 'I feel it here...
with you.'

'What?'

'I've cancelled my endoscopy. It's his name
that's been making me ill.'

'Oh...'

'So when you asked me to kiss you—yes, I
was surprised, but I was also very mindful that
you do not give away kisses. It was the most im-
practical kiss,' Galen said, 'given you were due
to start working for me, but...'

'Sympathy?'

He thought for a moment. 'I was trying to do
the right thing for you. It seemed right at the time.'
He looked at her then. 'I guess I was wrong.'

'No.'

'Then why can't you talk to me?'

He went inside, leaving her staring up at the
sky.

It was such a lovely night, and she could never
have nipped out and taken notes, for as she listened to the speeches his name was quite a regular occurrence.

Hector announced that the game was near completion and would be available in the New Year,
to thunderous applause.

'I can't wait!' Dora clapped the loudest.

Roula honestly was bemused. Did she not even know she'd been playing it all this time?

It would seem that this man did a lot of good in the world.

But a rather more hard-ass PA might be required for a man trying to set up a financial system that would work in an impoverished part of the planet. Or when society collapsed and fiat currency was worth nothing...

That brilliant brain, Roula thought.

They were all applauding as Hector returned to his seat, and she went out to the loo for a little cry and checked her phone.

Catch up later?

He had a nerve. That was her second thought. Her first was, *Yes, please.*

Except she'd be a terrible catch-up girl. She'd cry over Kupia Florakis, or confess her undying love, or admit that her period was late.

And so she didn't answer.

Galen didn't seem bothered by her lack of response.

'Hey, Dora, come and dance,' he said.

She watched as he danced with Dora. Clearly the ball was her night of nights.

Galen danced with all the women at the table, in fact, and Roula danced with Nico, and then had to make a dash away from him because she had a dreadful feeling that he was about to ask her out.

She gulped water.

'Come on,' Galen said, taking her hand. 'You haven't turned him down?'

'He hasn't asked yet.' She breathed out. 'I managed to get away.'

'We can dance two dances,' Galen said. 'I did three with Dora, two with the lady who smells of roses, so we have a clear run.'

'Good.'

'Can I ask you something?' Galen said, and he felt her stiffen in his arms.

'Of course,' she said.

'Do you think Hector and Dora…?'

'No…' She looked over and saw they were dancing. 'Maybe…'

'Please, no,' Galen said. 'It would be hell having them both pushing me for the next game.' Then he told her a something, that he hoped would show he trusted her more than anyone. 'She does deserve to be happy, though. Talk to Dora sometime.'

'I have.'

'Good.'

'She's going to ask you to send her on a business trip.' She draped her arm around his neck as they danced. 'I thought you were gamer boy?'

'I am.'

'Crypto kid?'

'That too.'

'I'm not coming back to your apartment.'

'So I'll make you come here.'

'Galen!'

'Yes,' he said. 'Can't you feel me?'

Roula said nothing.

'I can feel your breasts flat on my chest,' Galen said. 'Are they taped up?'

'No...' she smiled.

'They must be,' he said. 'Because this dress is backless, and they are very beautiful, but I can't feel...'

'I think the bra is inbuilt,' she said.

He put his hand in the small of her back, and her skin felt so warm she might have been standing in front of a fire before placing it there.

'Maybe dancing isn't so pointless,' he said.

'No...'

He dusted her arm with his fingers, as he had wanted to that night, and pulled her in closer. And he knew that for all the things he didn't get in this life, he *did* get Roula. Of that, he was sure.

'I knew you were about to cry on the beach,' Galen said into her ear. 'That's why I came over.'

She was very still.

'You do this thing with your hands and your eyes. And when you're upset you get angry...'

* * *

'Galen…' She felt as if she were being pulled apart even while held in his arms. This was a character assessment when she did not want scrutiny. But he held her in a way that she did not want to leave.

'I don't know what I've done,' he admitted. 'I can't work that out.'

'Good,' Roula said, for she did not want him to know how much she loved him.

'Our dance is over,' Galen said, and she heard the music still a little more gently than it had the night they had met, when Leo had crashed. 'History repeats itself.'

'Does it?'

'You went off into the night last time.'

'If it wasn't for Costa we'd never have seen each other again.'

'Believe what you want, Roula, but I'd have got in touch.'

'I said no to you.'

'Yes,' he agreed. 'And I respected that. But I knew something had been left undone…'

Roula swallowed. 'As I said, history repeats itself.'

They were back at the table.

'Come on Dora,' Galen said. 'One more.'

Roula was left with Hector, who was looking longingly at Dora.

Thankfully Nico had discovered someone from social media, who was now draped around him, and so Roula collected up her purse and knew she could leave.

The sensible part of her mind was reminding her that having this conversation with Galen might be better done from afar, because she really didn't want him to see her breaking down.

Except she felt ridiculously alive tonight.

On fire.

Brave, even.

So it was Roula who took out her phone and sat at the table as if butter wouldn't melt in her mouth and replied to his text.

Yes.

She got a smiley face in return.

CHAPTER EIGHTEEN

'YOU'LL HAVE TO close your eyes,' Galen said as he led her through the apartment. 'Your gift is in the bedroom.'

'What a surprise!' Roula said in a droll voice, but he came up behind her and his hand covered her eyes.

'I'm serious,' he said. 'I didn't have time to wrap them.'

'Them?' she checked.

'Just close your eyes.'

He led her into the bedroom and she stood there waiting—for what? A naked Galen? Gosh he made her thoughts depraved...

But she was not scared. It was odd, but even in the dark she wasn't frightened.

'Open them.'

'Wow!' Roula said, forcing a smile as she surveyed a new luggage set. Gosh, clearly Galen wasn't the King of Romance! 'It's beautiful.'

'Isn't it?' Galen said. 'They all come with a lifetime guarantee.'

She guessed in his own way he was giving her his blessing to leave. 'Thank you,' Roula said. 'I mean that. I'm...'

Underwhelmed.

Except she shouldn't be, Roula knew, for it was

the best luggage set ever, and he was the sexiest man in the world, and he was trying to make this right.

'I'm touched.'

Sort of.

Not.

She felt as if she'd got on a bus headed in the wrong direction, or on a ferry that was taking her to a port she didn't want to go to but had insisted upon. Everything was chugging along in the wrong direction, and she didn't know how to turn things around.

'Come here,' Galen said, and he took her hand and led her towards the terrace and the view she had missed the first time around.

She loved Athens, Roula thought as she stepped out onto the terrace. And, yes, Galen had the best view. For the Temple of Olympian Zeus was lit up in the foreground, so close, and high and proud behind it stood the Acropolis.

'Worth it?' he asked.

'So worth it,' Roula said, and even as she drank in the view her words were for him. 'You can never move,' she smiled. 'I mean, how would you top that?'

'I'm very lucky,' Galen said. 'I know that.'

'So am I,' Roula said, because tonight she felt so too. 'I never thought I'd be…' *Where to start?*

'Dancing, making new friends, firing off texts requesting sex!'

'It's such an effective method of communication.' He smiled. 'I'm teasing.'

She smiled as he took her arms in his hands,

'It's been a brilliant six weeks,' Galen said. 'Well, perhaps not for you.'

'It's been the very best that it could have been. I honestly thought I'd be facing it alone.'

Yes, she was minus a family, but she had a cast of new friends and a new sense of herself now. She was no longer Guest Services Manager Roula, the woman he'd first met, or PA Roula as she'd tried to be, or 'poor Roula', as some of them back home called her.

But neither was she the New Roula she'd tried so hard to create. The one who stood in a sexy ball gown and knew what to do and how to say goodbye.

'I don't want to cry,' she said.

'Tomorrow,' he said, and kissed her…softly at first.

Roula had guessed she was going to get gentle Galen, all tender, now that he knew the truth. Except she didn't know Galen, nor the way he could kiss her in full view of Athens.

He sucked at the tip of her tongue, just a bit, and then he sucked at her bottom lip. And then, when she thought she knew his kiss, he changed it. He kissed her so hard, so deep, that if the sky hadn't been navy then it might have turned pink, for he was devouring her with his mouth and then denying her his kiss.

They were right on the edge, looking at each other, almost challenging each other—to what, neither quite knew.

'Come inside,' he said.

She knew she must, or they would be arrested, or filmed, or who knew what.

He led her not to his bed, but to the most beautiful bathroom in the world.

'Are we having a bath?' she asked.

'Takes too long to fill,' Galen said. 'Maybe later.'

'I love your bathroom.'

'It's the best.'

She looked in the mirror and he stood behind her. 'Why are we in here?'

'So I can look at you,' Galen said. 'At us.'

He looked stunning, end-of-the-night beautiful, and somehow her dress looked even better in the soft antique mirror and she could admit something.

'It feels vain, but I think I look beautiful…' She couldn't stop looking—not so much at herself, more at *them*.

'Tonight, everyone is beautiful. Monday, not so much…' Galen said.

Roula did not want to think about Monday, and she didn't have to right now—because he was undoing the little hooks on her dress between deep kisses to her shoulder, and she watched his lips on her skin and the gentle suck of his mouth. Every now and then the hooks irritated him, so he gave in and pressed his hands into her breasts, kissed her neck as she watched.

'I don't want to leave a mark,' he said, getting back to the little clasps. 'Not a good look for your first day at work.'

She flushed with tense anger as he brought up Monday again, when they would be no more, but then he dealt with the last clasp and exposed her breasts.

Roula stared at them, all white and creamy, and the ridiculous thing was it was as if she had never really seen them before—well, at least not until Galen. She had just stuffed them into a bra. Now they fascinated her. He was stroking them from behind and his head was lowering, so she could only see his hands. He kissed the notches at the top of her spine, and then her scapula as if it was the most vital part of her. She had barely known it existed, let alone that his mouth upon it might make her want to fold over.

'I've wanted to do that all night,' he said, coming up to stand. 'And this...' Galen said, and he helped her step out of the dress so she stood only in lacy knickers and heels.

'Look,' he told her.

'Galen…'

She was the only one near naked, and she knew it would be a whole lot easier to be buried in his kiss than to confront the sight of herself in the mirror. 'Galen behind glass,' she said, looking at his hands on her stomach. His fingers were creeping into the lace, and she told him one of her secrets. 'I touched myself once, thinking about you.'

'Did you?'

Roula nodded. 'Before…'

'I like knowing that.' He was kissing the skin between her neck and her shoulder.

'I didn't know what I was doing.'

'Show me.' He took her hand and he guided it down, and his hand was over hers.

'It was one morning,' she said. 'I pictured you in uniform.'

'Did you do it like this?' he asked, taking her finger and making it stroke her slowly.

'No…' She was upended with the memory of a kiss that didn't exist, of how it had felt when the only desire she'd known was Galen. 'Like this.'

She turned, and now it was Roula leading, undoing his buttons just to get to his skin, kissing him as she had wanted to then. Hungry, desperate kisses. And even if her mouth didn't know what to do, it worked, because he met her as she climbed up him and gathered her in.

His tongue was duelling with hers as he tore her brand-new knickers. She was at his neck now, feeling the slap of his belt coming undone on her inner thigh, and then he guided her onto him.

'Look,' he told her.

And she rested her head on his shoulder and watched his taut buttocks in the mirror as he thrust in. Her breasts were flat against him and her hair was falling down.

'My turn,' he said.

She felt the cold of marble on her bottom. Galen was looking down on them and very slowly he took her, stroking her curls, playing with her, and Roula could see her own thighs shaking.

'Slowly,' he said, and then he swore, and his hand went for the cabinet behind her.

They were giving in. They were having the sex they should have had way back then, because now they were beyond sensible.

'You're really bad for me, Roula.'

'I know.' She was coming just a little, right on the edge of it, and just so fascinated by him…by them, by the absolute freedom he allowed her. 'I want to see you come,' she told him.

'Shh…' Galen said, because he was doing all he could not to do that.

'I want to.' Her voice was rising, urgent—imperative.

As he swelled he pulled out, and she glimpsed the brief pulse of his come, and then he slid back into her and she folded. Dizzy and frantic, she came so deeply that he gathered her in, his hands warm on her bottom, as she gripped the last of him.

And then, drunk on pleasure, they kissed each other all the way to bed, and she lay there so happy and watched him undress.

'You have to hang your dress up,' he said as he looked at her.

'No...'

'You do,' he told her. 'I don't want Leo telling us off. Go on.'

'No!'

But she was laughing, reluctant, obliging, hanging up her dress. And it was the nicest moment as she realised she could laugh, and that her night with Galen wasn't over.

They weren't done with the other yet.

Floating. That was exactly what it was. Just as Galen had described it.

'What are you thinking?' he asked, and she knew he never usually did.

'That I haven't checked in for my flight,' Roula lied. 'You?'

* * *

That you're pregnant, and yet you can't tell me.

Galen was certain now. And not just from the changes in her body…

But what caused the real disquiet was the fact that he was certain she knew, too.

He was certain she was terrified, and perhaps that was why she was running away.

Perhaps she didn't want him to know, Galen considered, and who could blame her?

Maybe she wanted freedom after the hell of her marriage.

'Charts?' she said, and he dragged his mind back to their little in-joke.

'Actually, I was just thinking that you didn't open all your present.'

'I did.'

'There's a handbag,' Galen said.

'Oh, yes?'

'To go with the luggage.'

'Thank you,' Roula said. 'That's really thoughtful.'

Perhaps there were flags and bunting in one of the cases, Roula thought, and a goodbye card signed by all the staff.

As Roula lay there she kept wanting to poke him, because she had loathed his quiet anger at her leaving, and yet she was opposed to his nonchalance.

She drifted off—only it wasn't her usual nightmare that jolted her awake, but the thought of a world without him.

She listened to his soft snores. How could he be asleep when she was leaving?

She waited for dawn before prodding him awake. 'Galen? I don't know if I want the job.'

'Why?'

'It's all happened too fast.'

'Not really.'

'Too much too soon.'

'I get that.' He pulled her in, blinking himself awake. 'Any other reason?'

'I love Athens.' Roula lay back with him. 'I didn't expect to fall in love with a city, but I think I have.'

'I fell in love with it too,' Galen said. 'It just blew me away. But you might feel the same in another city.'

'Yes…'

'So what else is tearing you up?'

'Yaya,' she said. 'I feel I let you down with her.'

'No, I told you—you've helped.'

Oh, she preferred him cross and sulking, or at least putting up a little resistance to her leaving, but it would seem Galen had made his peace with it.

'Any other concerns?' he asked. 'Because now is the time to air them.'

'You said that at our first dinner.'

'Yes,' he agreed. 'I remember—and you asked me to kiss you.'

Roula groaned, and wished she had the energy to cover her face with the sheet that was crumpled around them.

'Say it, Roula.'

'Okay,' she took a breath. 'I do have a concern.' Although she truly did not know how to share her troubles. 'Us,' she admitted.

'Us?' He turned and looked at her.

'I know there's not supposed to be an "us", and I know I really am the worst catch-up girl, but I just thought…'

'What?'

'That I wanted sex—and I did. But…' She blew out a breath. 'You're right…we were just getting good.'

'Yes.'

She screwed her eyes closed. 'And it's just…'

'What?'

'I have feelings for you.'

'I have feelings for you too.'

'I have a *lot* of feelings for you, Galen,' Roula said.

'How many are we talking?'

'I'm not sure,' she said. 'Quite a lot.'

'Roula,' he said, 'I'm going to get coffee and some pastries.'

Not the reaction she'd hoped for!

He was gone for ages and she lay there, the neediest catch-up girl in the world. But if she couldn't tell him she was crazy about him on her last full day in Athens, then when? And not just head over heels in love with him, Roula thought, biting the skin around her thumb, but very possibly pregnant too!

She didn't know what to do. Truly. So she wrapped the sheet around her and went into the kitchen to get a drink of water, grateful for a quiet stomach, and for the fact that she wasn't head-down in the loo this morning.

His kitchen was gleaming, a chef's dream, and entirely wasted on Galen, who probably didn't even know how to turn on the kettle.

She was going to cry, Roula knew, so she clenched her fists and looked up—and then caught her breath when she saw the ceiling... not so perfect after all.

'Shocking, isn't it?'

She turned as Galen came in and looked up at the sooty ceiling and wall and the terrible scorch marks.

'When did this fire happen?' Roula asked.

'Ten...twelve years ago.' Galen shrugged. 'When I first moved in.'

'And you haven't had it repainted?'

'Why would I?' he said. 'It's just another de-signer kitchen without it.' He grinned and looked up. 'You can almost see Costa's panic, knowing I was on the plane on my way back. It happened. I like it.'

He held up a paper bag that looked full of greasy goodies and a tray with two cups.

'Breakfast in bed.'

Roula wandered back into the bedroom and climbed onto the bed, feeling a bit sick now—but with nerves.

'Coffee?' he said.

'No thanks.' The thought made her stomach curdle.

'Tea, then,' he said. 'Mint tea.'

'Oh!' She perked up a bit. 'Thank you.'

'Roula,' Galen said. 'It was very brave of you to just do what you did. I mean that.'

'Thank you.'

'We *do* have feelings for each other, but...'

It was like one of those job rejection letters, Roula thought. *Dear Ms Drakos, Thank you for your application, but...*

'You still haven't opened all of your present.' He handed her the handbag. 'There's something inside.'

A coin, probably. Or some lucky charm.

'Thanks.'

There was a sliver of velvet inside.

'Open it,' Galen said.

And when she unrolled it Roula found the pure sound of silence in Athens, for there were no words from her. It was a thin gold chain with a cross.

'This was...' he started.

'Your mother's,' she said.

'Yes,' Galen said. 'And I'm giving it to you.'

'As a leaving present?'

'No, because I love you.'

'You don't.'

'Roula, I completely do. And it's very important that you get that. I love you, and I feel sick at the thought of you leaving, but if you want to go to London I'll come too.'

She looked at him and frowned.

'After Yaya's dead.'

God, he was blunt sometimes. 'I don't think London's the issue...' she began.

'No, but are we clear? I love you.'

'I think so,' she said, because she was lifting her hair and he was putting the gold chain on her, his most precious thing.

'Know so,' Galen said. 'I love you because you are everything. You are strong and brave and...'

'Galen, I'm not brave.'

'You are.'

'I'm terrified.'

'Of what?'

He lifted her chin and his amber gaze met hers, held hers… And, yes, she was nervous, and worried, but more noticeable than that was the absence of fear. It was as if the terror that had resided in her heart had simply exited, and now she looked back at the man she trusted, with all her heart.

Even the wobbly bits.

Even the scary bits that might blow up their plans and change their lives.

For the first time in as long as Roula could remember, she believed that she wasn't on her own.

Yes, there might be an issue, but she didn't have to face things alone.

'My period's a bit late,' she said.

'How late are we talking?' Galen asked.

'Late!' Roula said. 'Quite late, actually.'

'Have you done a test?'

'No.'

'Why not?'

'I don't want to know.'

'Well, I do.' He handed her a paper cup. 'Go and pee in that.'

'Pardon?'

'I bought a test this morning. We'll deal with facts.'

'But I can't have babies.'

'Who told you that?' he said. 'A qualified fertility specialist?'

He tried to rein in his contempt, but he did know a little bit about it—not that he'd tell her about Kristina and Ruben's battles. Somehow he could not picture Roula and him sitting nervously, holding hands in a waiting room, awaiting results.

'On a trip to Athens to check if anything was wrong?'

'No...' She shook her head. 'I feel so naive.'

'And I feel I let you down.'

'No.'

'Roula, go and pee.'

She took a breath as she climbed out of bed.

He caught her wrist. 'I love you.'

'Stop...' She shook her head. 'You're just saying that in case I am...'

'Roula, why would I say it?'

'I've trapped you.'

'How?' he demanded. 'I can have only monthly access, send a card now and then, pay you maintenance—we have a lot of choices.'

'Do we?'

'Loads. And if you want London I have a very mobile job...' He took back the cup from her hand, and although he wanted to know, there were more important things than facts. 'If you are pregnant, will *you* feel trapped?'

'Galen...'

She flashed him a smile. He wasn't sure which one—her guest services manager smile, her fake PA smile, her new Roula smile? Anyway it died on her lips. How did she feel?

'Roula? How do you feel?'

'Better than I did a few days ago,' she said. 'What about you?'

'We're talking about how *you* feel.'

'If I am pregnant, then I want to be—with or without you. Because I want honesty more than I want you, Galen. I mean that. I would rather you kept your catch-up list and we did this apart than be in a relationship the other didn't want.'

'You want my truth?'

'Yes.'

'In my old ideal world,' Galen said, 'we would have had sex for two selfish years and then perhaps talked about babies. But I am surprisingly open to persuasion here. I don't know when I fell in love, but I think it's been the case for quite some time. I know you won't believe this, but even before Costa asked me to employ you I was considering staying on the island. It grew from there. And you can call me arrogant again, but I think you might love me.'

'I do.'

'Since when?' Galen asked, pleased at her honesty.

'Always,' Roula said. 'Not like this, of course,

but I cried when you left, and you know I had a crush on you, but…' She looked at him. 'I wondered if you ever thought of me,' she admitted. 'Not all the time, just now and then. I would look back on times when I'd been happy, and most of those times included you.'

And then for Galen it all slotted into place—her anger, her hurt, all aimed towards him.

'I did let you down, then.'

'How could you when you didn't know?'

'No,' Galen said, 'but I'm finding out that love is very illogical.' He meant what he said next. 'I'm so sorry I wasn't there for you.'

'It wasn't even the real you I had a crush on, Galen.' Although it felt as if she had loved him all her life.

'Go and get your bag,' he said. When she didn't move, Galen got it for her. He took out her Dictaphone and fiddled with it for a moment. 'Press "Play".'

'Why?'

'I recorded a message last night. You were meant to hear it today, when you typed up the notes. Press "Play".'

'Roula…'

His voice was low and there was music playing in the background. She knew the very moment, because she'd been standing in the loo, reading his message.

'I don't come with a ring, but there is a present in a handbag which I think should tell you how much you mean to me. Can we talk before you go? Because I think I am falling in love with you.'

'You are romantic after all!'

'See?' He gave her a nice smile. 'I had it all planned. And then I saw your amazing bust and…' He looked down at her stomach and then up to her eyes. 'We can decide now that we'll always be together. Whatever that pregnancy test says.'

It was time to find out.

She walked into the bathroom and did what she must, and then came back to the bedroom, where he'd opened the drapes. And there was the very best view.

'Where's the test?' she asked.

'I'll do it,' Galen said. 'Drink your tea.'

But not even mint tea and the sunrise and the Acropolis could distract her, for she turned around and he was like some naked Greek god in the bathroom, standing with his back to her, as if he was doing a scientific experiment with a pipette, when really he should just dunk it in.

She could see his expression.

His eyes were on the stick.

She'd have three minutes of this—or was it five? He would feel her looking soon and fake a smile.

But then she looked at the mirrors. They were cracked, and rather than fix them he adored them and didn't hide the cracks. And she thought of the sooty ceiling that he kept, rather than paint over, because it made him smile. Then she caught her own reflection in the damaged mirror, saw herself sitting on the bed, and the chain around her neck, and she thought of that line she had held on to.

And I will restore to you the years that the locust hath eaten.

And she wasn't scared because this really was love, she knew. Real love. Coming now…ready or not.

'Roula!'

She heard his excited shout. It was so absolute she jumped.

'You're pregnant!'

It was as if they had been trying for five years, and yet they had not even been trying. Galen was swearing and panicking and delighted.

She was in love, and pregnant, and as he kissed her all over there was just one more thing—and he'd made her brave enough to say it. To state her needs upfront.

'I want a ring, Galen.'

He stopped mid-kiss.

'And a wedding,' Roula said.

'Roula, I have very strong opinions—'

'Well, I don't want to be Roula Kyrios or Roula Dra—'

'Marry me,' he said hurriedly—because that name would never be said in this bedroom. 'It would seem I do believe in marriage after all.'

And the most illogical thing was that as he got down on one knee he actually did.

CHAPTER NINETEEN

MIST OVER THE AEGEAN, Galen thought as she walked out of the bedroom. And for all the reasons he loved her—and there were many—one of them was because she wore that gorgeous dress all over again.

It really was perfect.

And so were they as he drove them to their wedding.

'Oh, my God!' Leo was dancing on the street as Roula climbed out, holding a cascade of vivid pink bougainvillea. 'She's wearing *me*!'

Galen was in the same wedding suit he had worn for Costa and Mary's wedding. They were there too. But no one knew his and Roula's secret just yet.

'Should we...?' Mary suggested, indicating that they go in.

'Or maybe...' Leo held back.

Costa just stood there, leaving it all to the others.

'I have spoken with the staff...' Kristina started, but Ruben, holding the baby, hushed her.

'Let them...'

'Thanks.' Galen nodded, because this wedding no one had been able to organise. This was a wedding arranged quickly, because—well, some things needed to be done rapidly.

'We'll call you in soon,' Galen said. 'Ready?' he checked with his bride-to-be.

'I am. Are you?'

He took a breath and nodded as they stepped in and walked along the hall.

Roula's breath caught, because one of the residents of the care home was playing the piano, and all of them were dressed in their finery. Diamonds and jewels and a very smart gentleman holding up a stick.

'Galen!'

'Sir,' Galen said, and this time he went over. 'Thank you for your help organising the guests. Everybody looks amazing.'

'Well, it's a wedding.'

'Yes, it is!'

It really was.

'Can I correct something?' Galen said, just before they went in.

'Of course,' Roula said.

'What I said about us having a baby in two years or so… I want to amend that. *Now* is ideal.'

'It is,' Roula agreed, because she was safe in his love now.

But there was another love that needed him too.

'Hey, Yaya...' He gently shook her and she opened her eyes.

'Home,' she said, when she saw the bright pink flowers.

'They *are* from home,' Galen said. 'Picked this morning, trailing down from your roof...'

'Galen...' She breathed in the scent and then looked up at Roula. 'Oh, you look like a bride.'

'Roula *is* my bride,' Galen said. 'The celebrant is here, and when you're ready we would like you to see us marry.'

'Galen!' She was tearful. 'Married?'

'Yes.' He nodded. 'I am in love, Yaya, and it would seem she loves me.'

'Good, good...'

'And,' he told her, 'no one else knows this yet, but we're having a baby.'

'Before marriage?'

'We're sorting that out right now. We're having a little girl.'

Sometimes it was better to lie, because it was actually a little too early to be sure.

'We're going to call her Constantina.' Roula told her what Galen could not, for today there was no need for pretence. 'After Galen's mother—and it's your middle name too.'

'Yes...'

'Yes,' Galen said, and then in front of these two women he cried. 'I remember everything you ever told me about her. I love because of you. The best *yaya*, the best parent—you are everything I want to be for my child. You loved little robot me.'

'Horrible boys,' she said, just as she had then. 'Clever you are.'

'I have been blessed to have you.'

It was the shortest, the sweetest wedding, in a room full of Anapliró memories and love, toasted in Anapliró water with a very light sponge cake and just a little smear of fig jam.

'Constantina…' Yaya beamed.

'Yes!' Roula smiled.

'Honeymoon?'

'We're saving it for Christmas,' Galen told her. 'We're going home to have the baby.'

'Home?'

'Our Anapliró home.'

It would not be dissolving into the sea.

EPILOGUE

'WOW…' SAID ROULA.

They sat on the steps of the *theatron*, gazing down on the world.

They were on their way back from Athens and had just visited her mother, for a little meet-and-greet. It had been emotional, but had gone surprisingly well. Then, as they'd been driving up to their Anapliró home, Roula had suggested they stop.

Galen had put a few flowers from a pink bouquet into his parents' *kandylakia*. The candle was still lit.

'Yes, wow,' Galen said.

Only Galen was wowed by little blue eyes and a very red face, all of a week old.

Roula would not be snapping back quite as quickly as Kristina, but she'd been able to take a gentle walk with their very precious wrapped bundle, and now they sat on the steps of what was the best place on earth to share their happy news.

Leo and Deacon, and Costa and Mary—with little Costa, of course—had dropped everything to visit them at the hospital. Kristina had been in too. As well as Dora and Hector! But there were plenty more they were ready to reveal the details to.

'I have a phone signal,' Roula declared.

'Tell them,' Galen said, not taking his eyes off his daughter.

It was quite a group message—especially for two people who had no real family.

Yolanda and Stephanie, and then there was Joe and Nico, and the guys on the ground floor… And really, for someone as supposedly socially backward as Galen, there was a very long list of essential people all waiting for their first glimpse of Constantina Pallas.

It took for ever to send the message—for *ever*—and they sat gazing down at their daughter. A little late, a little bit of a worry, a whole lot to love.

'A whole person…' Galen just stared at her. 'Condensed!'

'I know!' Roula agreed. 'I mean, she's everything—an entire person. Yet this tiny little fragile creature at the same time.'

She got him.

'Home?' Galen said.

Up to their Anapliró home, to get to know their little girl. For he got her too, and home, with their little family, was where her heart was right now.

Galen knew Roula.

* * * * *